D0230586

Chapter 1

I lean over the rail, looking down at jagged rocks where waves crash and break. Plumes of spray blow away in the wind.

"Would they even notice if I was gone?" I whisper into the breeze.

The band finishes their song and the sound of applause ripples across the lush gardens. I know I should go back inside, but I'm still coming to terms with how things have changed.

Looking in through the window, I see my dad dancing with Maggie, his new wife. His face is alight with happiness, and I hardly recognize him. It makes me realize that he hasn't been truly happy since my mom died.

I haven't either.

She was the anchor that held our family secure

– Dad, Susan, Todd and me. Without her, the storms of life blew us apart. Susan and Todd left home but, as the youngest, I stayed on the ranch with Dad, both of us just trying to survive.

And now there's Maggie, and Dad looks complete again. But where does that leave me?

The wind catches the edge of my dress and swirls it around my legs. It's a gorgeous ocean blue chiffon, but it feels alien to me. I never wear dresses. They're no good for riding and right now, I long for my jeans and riding boots. I long for my Appaloosa stallion, Blue, and the open pastures of our ranch in Idaho. If I could only ride away right now …

I turn back to the ocean, tears in my eyes.

"Jenna, come in and dance!" my sister Susan calls from the door where the wedding reception is in full swing.

I brush the tears away. "Coming, sis."

On the way in, I grab another double vodka and coke. I don't usually drink much but tonight, I need some help to get through. Another one won't hurt.

It's late now and the band is nearly finished. I plaster a smile on my face as I dance with Susan and my two little nieces. I can't believe they're not in bed, but I guess tonight is special and they're loving the party. Harry, Maggie's son, is dancing with his sister, Samantha and her husband, Luke. A blonde girl, Lizzie Martin, dances nearby with her brother, Dan, and they laugh as he spins her around.

The British contingent.

I guess they are part of the family now, but their accents and perfect manners make me feel like a ranch hand. The Martins are close family friends of Maggie's from her village of Summerfield. The name conjures up quaint cottages, white picket fences, neat rosebushes, and cucumber sandwiches. Give me the wild forests of Idaho any day.

I look over at Dad and Maggie, wrapped in each other's arms, eyes only for one another. It's hard to remember him ever looking at Mom like that, but he must have, once upon a time.

Will a man ever gaze at me that way?

The band finishes their song, and after applause, the leader announces, "Ladies and gentlemen, the bride and groom!"

Everyone claps again as Dad and Maggie make their way around the room, saying their goodbyes. They're going to New Zealand on a honeymoon trip that sounds magical. I've never traveled anywhere. My life has revolved around the ranch and my horses, but I'm starting to wonder how much more is out there.

I hover near the door. Maggie and I had a rocky start to our friendship. I pretty much tried to drown her, but I apologized and I think we're okay now. I can't bear to see them go. I grab another double vodka and gulp it down. It burns my throat, but the warmth helps as Dad comes up and hugs me.

"I love you, Jenn." He holds me so tight that I can hardly breathe and I understand how much more he wants to say, but he never will. My dad, Greg Warren, is a mountain man, as staunch and silent as the Rockies. He pulls away. "Be safe now."

Maggie stands next to Dad, her eyes shining. Although they are both older, tonight, they look young again. She reaches out her hands to me, and I take them.

"Thanks for coming, Jenna," she whispers.

"Maggie, I'm sorry I –"

She shakes her head and kisses me on the cheek. "It's in the past now. Let's begin again."

"Have a great honeymoon."

Dad and Maggie join hands as confetti rains down upon them. They run to the wedding limo and wave goodbye from the back window. As the car turns the corner, they are lost from sight. I stand for a moment staring after them.

"Are you okay?" The English accent is crisp, and I turn to find Dan Martin next to me. He's taller than me, but only just, and I'm tall. I notice that his nose is slightly crooked, an old sporting injury

Penny Appleton

Love Will
Find A Way

A Summerfield Village
sweet romance

This book is a work of fiction. The characters, incidents and dialogue are drawn from the author's imagination and are not to be construed as real. Any resemblance to actual events or persons, living or dead, is fictionalized or coincidental.

Love Will Find A Way
Copyright © Penny Appleton (2017). All rights reserved.

www.PennyAppleton.com

ISBN: 978-1-912105-82-3

The right of Penny Appleton to be identified as the author of this work has
been asserted by the author in accordance with the Copyright, Designs and Patents Act,1988. All rights reserved. No part of this publication may be reproduced, stored in a retrieval system, or transmitted, in any form, or by any means, electronic, mechanical, photocopying, recording or otherwise, without the prior permission of the publishers.

This book is sold subject to the condition that it shall not, by way of trade or otherwise, be lent, resold, hired out, or otherwise circulated without the author's prior consent in any form of binding or cover other than that in which it is published and without a similar condition being imposed on the subsequent purchaser.

Requests to publish work from this book should be sent to:
penny@pennyappleton.com

Cover and Interior Design: JD Smith Design

www.CurlUpPress.com

Printed by CreateSpace

perhaps? His dark eyes are concerned, and I find myself gazing into them for just a little too long. "Jenna?"

"Yes, thanks. I'm fine. Just getting another drink."

I walk away and leave him there. I don't want to talk to him, or anyone else. More vodka will help finish the night and I need some air.

But as I walk away, I find myself wobbling.

The room spins. A cold sweat prickles my skin. My stomach tightens.

A door nearby opens onto the patio and I dash through. Falling to my knees, spasms rock through me and I vomit into the flowerbed.

A gentle hand holds my hair away from my face. "It's okay. Let it all out." Dan squats next to me and hands me a linen napkin with a bottle of water. "Sip this. It will make you feel better."

I turn to sit on a low stone wall, utterly embarrassed, but at the same time, so grateful for his help. My head is spinning, and it feels like I might throw up again.

I rub my aching stomach. "I'm sorry you had to see that."

"I'm sure today has been tough for you," Dan says, quietly. "And I understand all about alcohol poisoning." He looks back through the windows where a woman with wild red hair waltzes alone on the dance floor. It's his mother, Christine, one of Maggie's friends. Something in his voice makes me realize that I'm not the only one with a troubled family.

I shiver as the wind from the ocean sweeps around us, swinging the colored lanterns and casting shadows across the lawn.

Dan pulls off his jacket and wraps it around my shoulders. "Here, you need to stay warm. Do you want to go back inside?"

I shake my head. "No, I don't want my sister or Aunt Barb to see me, I'll only get a lecture. To be honest, I don't party much. I'm just a cowgirl from Boise, Idaho."

Dan raises an eyebrow. "Ah, home of the famous Idaho potatoes."

"It's the only thing you Brits know about Idaho! But it has a lot more going for it than potatoes." I nudge him in mock annoyance.

He laughs, and suddenly, I don't feel so alone. I turn to him, mesmerized by his hazel eyes. They remind me of a summer dawn in the Boise foothills.

"Tell me about where you come from. Where is your home?"

"I live in Summerfield village, near Oxford in the south of England," he begins. I lose myself in his warm voice as he speaks of his family farm, of fields and apple orchards, cascading blossom in the spring. He takes me walking through woods with bluebells and soft English rain. He talks of the barns and gardens around their rambling old farmhouse, and horses galloping in the fields for pure joy.

"Horses?" I ask, breaking the spell.

Dan nods. "My mother breeds Welsh Mountain show ponies. I did dressage and had a wonderful horse, Royal Connection. But Mum sold him when I went to Scotland to train as a teacher. There's not much time to ride, working full time in a classroom. Maggie said that you ride, too?"

Thoughts of Blue and his herd wash over me. "Yes." I blink furiously, trying to hold back the tears. "I wish I was home with my horses right now." If I start to cry, I don't think I'll ever stop.

"I'm feeling a bit better now. Could we walk down to the water's edge and get some more fresh air? I don't want to go back in to the party."

Dan stands and reaches down to help me. His hands are strong and capable and he notices the matching calluses on our palms.

"We both have riding and working hands." He smiles and tucks my hand through his arm, helping me down the path to a tiny sheltered bay. Gentle waves whisper in across the sand, and we sit on smooth rocks.

Dan is silhouetted against bright stars, looking out over the ocean. There's a dark shadow of stubble on his chin. He's motionless, taking it all in. The gentle whoosh of the ocean and our breathing are the only sounds.

He hands me the half-empty bottle of water. "You should keep drinking this. You'll appreciate it in the morning."

I take a sip. "What made you become a teacher?"

"I like kids and I want to make a difference. Sixth grade kids are challenging, but they have such enthusiasm. I get a huge kick out of working with them. I helped Mum with her pony club when I was a teenager, and I was a fair dressage rider. But she and I have our difficulties and we clash, maybe like you do with your dad." He smiles. "Mum thinks I'm better at things than I am, but it was her ambition to be an Olympic rider, not mine. We need to follow our own dreams. Teaching is my vocation, not just a job. What about you, Jenna, what are you passionate about?"

I pause for a moment. I've never really questioned what I want to do with my life, it has just turned out the way it has. But I love our ranch and the horses, so I can't imagine being anywhere else.

"I'm passionate about saving Appaloosa horses and I love working on the ranch." I look out at the ocean. "It's a long way from here to Boise and quite different in Idaho. I help our foreman with the stock and manage the horses for two ranches, Doug's and ours. I particularly love working with Barb, rescuing abandoned or abused horses."

"Is Barb Greg's sister? Maggie mentioned how welcoming she was."

"She's not my real aunt, but I've known her all my life. She's … she was …" I take a deep breath. "She was my mom's best friend, but my mom is dead."

I can't help but cry. Dan wraps his arms around me and pulls me close. The tears soak his shirt.

"I miss her so much."

Dan sighs. "My parents separated just before Lizzie was born and my dad went back to Australia. I was young and don't remember him very well." He pauses, and I wonder what he's holding back. "I know it's not the same, but I have some idea of what it feels like to lose a parent."

He hugs me closer and I wrap my arms around his waist. I'm suddenly aware of the taut muscles in his stomach, and the musky scent of him in the dark. Sympathy shifts to something else between us, the air almost crackling.

Dan pulls away suddenly. "We should go."

Losing his warmth leaves me cold and shivering

on the rock. He puts out a hand. "I'll walk you back to your room."

A spark of hope flickers within me. Maybe he will come inside and hold me? I've had flirtations with men before, but nothing serious since my crush on Calvin Wilson, Boise's golden boy. But he was never interested in me. Perhaps Dan can see past the cowgirl to the woman beneath.

When we get to my room, I turn and put both arms around him.

"Dan," I whisper, "I'm lonely. Would you come in?"

He hugs me close and strokes my hair. I'm trembling, and I desperately want him to kiss me.

"Jenna, you are a beautiful woman, but you've had too much to drink." He takes a deep breath. "And you might not even remember tonight in the morning. I'm flying back to England tomorrow to spend Christmas with my family. Then I leave for a job in Australia. You and I … well, it can't go anywhere, and I won't take advantage of you."

His words shake me and I can't speak. He kisses the top of my head.

"Goodnight, Jenna." He walks away down the corridor and I watch him go. Finally, I meet a man I'm seriously attracted to. Can this be over before it's even begun?

Chapter 2

The loud buzzing of the hotel phone wakes me. Bright sunlight streams through the curtains, and I squint, groaning as I turn over. My head is pounding, but not as badly as it might have been. I remember Dan's face in the dark, his arms around me and I want to stay in that dream …

But the phone doesn't stop.

I pull it toward me.

"Jenna, come and have breakfast with us." Barb's voice is way too cheery for the morning after a wedding. "Hurry up, Susan and the girls are here too."

I stifle a groan. Sky and Shelby will probably want to play, and the thought of their excited squealing makes me think twice about going to breakfast at all.

But Dan might be there.

"On my way."

I shower quickly and then look in the mirror. The blue chiffon dress and professional make-up of yesterday are gone, leaving plain Jenna Warren, Boise cowgirl. I scarcely notice my appearance on the ranch. It's more about functionality than beauty. After all, who do I have to be beautiful for?

But I might bump into Dan at breakfast …

I twist my long black hair up and clip it into a knot, leaving part of it falling as a ponytail. I find a clean t-shirt and my least crumpled jeans. It's the best I can do. I take a deep breath and head downstairs.

Barb and Doug sit with my sister and nieces in the dining room, and they wave as I walk in. Then I see Dan sitting at a table near the window. My heart beats faster.

He looks up and smiles as I approach.

"Morning, Jenna." He stands up, pushing back his chair, and kisses my cheek. I've seen other Europeans greet each other this way. It doesn't mean anything, but do his lips linger just a touch too long for a new friend?

"Good morning."

"How are you feeling?"

"Much better for your help, thank you." I notice the coffee pot and crumbs, his laptop open beside him. "Did you have breakfast already?"

"Yes. I ate with Harry, Samantha, and Luke. They're on an early flight back to London. Your brother Todd was on the shuttle too. But my family haven't emerged yet, they're on a flight late this afternoon.." He pauses. "I was hoping to see you before I left."

"When are you leaving?"

"On the shuttle in an hour. But I'm going for a quick walk on the beach before I go. San Diego weather at this time of year is a lot better than England." He grins. "I wish I could stay longer, but I'm in charge of the children's Nativity play at our church. I need to be back for the last rehearsals."

"You can't let the kids down." I smile, but inside, I'm disappointed. "When are you going to Australia?"

"Right after Christmas. How about giving me your email and I'll send you a picture of a kangaroo."

I giggle and jump at the chance to stay in touch. We swap email and phone details. Susan is waving at me from their table, Sky and Shelby jumping around beside her. They look as if they will launch themselves at me if I delay any longer.

"I'd better go."

Dan nods. "I'll come back and say goodbye before I leave, if you're still here."

"I'll be here."

Where else would I be? He packs up his things as I walk over to my family.

"Can we go in the pool, Jenna?" Sky tugs at my arm. "Can we? Can we?"

It's a perfect day outside. The sun glints off the ocean, and gulls cry overhead. A swim sounds good. Maybe it will wash away thoughts of Dan and what might have been.

"Just let me have some breakfast." I give my nieces a hug, and they run outside to play, followed by an ever-patient Susan.

"Was that Dan Martin you were talking to?" Barb asks, nonchalantly.

Doug looks over the sports pages of the paper at her, one eyebrow raised at her tone. Then he looks at me and I can't help the blush rising on my cheeks. I dive into the menu, ordering a fresh mango smoothie and a mushroom omelet.

"I think he's going on the next shuttle," Barb continues. "It's amazing to think of all the people here, traveling back home again today. Such a big world we live in."

I suddenly wish that I was going off for an adventure, not home to Idaho. My life at the ranch seems so mundane. I'd miss Blue, but I've never traveled much farther than Seattle. No wonder Dan can only see a ranch girl. He probably knows a lot of sophisticated, well-traveled women in England.

The waiter brings my smoothie, and I take a long sip, the cool juice soothing my raw throat.

"Oh, Jenna, I almost forgot. Your dad and Maggie left you this." Barb pulls out a rectangular box wrapped in gold paper. It's the size of a book. I certainly like reading, but it seems an odd present right now.

I peel off the paper and open the box inside. Wrapped in deep blue tissue paper is a new credit card with my name on it, two keys on a brushed steel fob, and a sealed envelope. I frown. What could these keys be for?

I turn over the fob. There's an etching on the back, a little square cottage with roses around the door.

"Land sakes," Barb exclaims. "Maggie's given you keys to her cottage in England."

I can't help but smile. Dad has told me how much Maggie's cottage means to her, and this shows that she's accepted me as one of her family.

"Open the envelope," Barb urges me.

I open it to find a beautiful Christmas card with Dad's writing inside.

Merry Christmas, Jenna.

Enclosed is a travel credit card. It's loaded with your wages for the years that you have worked on the ranch with me. I've needed your help for so long, and you've been an incredible daughter and friend.

Now, I hope that you will take some time for yourself. Doug and Barb will look after the ranch, so you don't need to worry about any of that. Take care of yourself.

Love you,

Dad xxx

I glance at Barb, and a lump comes to my throat. She smiles reassuringly, and I read on, holding tight to my emotions. Maggie has written underneath.

Dear Jenna,

Happy Christmas! Samantha and Harry have keys to Square Cottage, my much-loved home in Summerfield. You are now my family too, so these are your keys. If you go traveling, you might enjoy staying there for a bit.

Happy New Year and I hope we can be better friends in the future.

Love, Maggie xxx

I'm bowled over by all the possibilities and wordlessly hand the card to Barb. She reads it and shakes her head, smiling broadly. Then she passes it to Doug.

"That's so exciting, Jenna. What will you do?"

"I … I don't know. I love the ranch. I've never really thought seriously about changing anything or traveling. But everything is different now, isn't it?"

"You have a lot more choices, that's for sure." Barb points to the credit card. "And I think your dad's encouraging you to go see the world, like he did."

Anxiety twists in my stomach. "But what if I don't want to go?"

Doug pats my arm. "You're so like Greg. You take your time to work things out. Trying to make you do anything always gets the opposite reaction. Todd's a bit like that, too."

"Not Susan?"

Barb shakes her head. "No, Susan's an old soul, like your mom was. Susan already knew about life when she was born."

I roll my eyes. My perfect big sister. "Lucky Susan."

Barb looks out into the garden. "She has her own challenges, Jenna. She and Steve are having difficulties, you know that, but she manages on her own. She doesn't talk to us much, she never did. But you

–" She reaches out a hand to clasp mine. "We were never lucky enough to have kids of our own, so when you were born, we told Rachel and Greg that maybe you could be half ours. You certainly spent half your childhood with us."

"We love you, Jenn." Doug smiles at me. "We'll miss you if you choose not to come home right now. Blue will too."

Barb squeezes my hand. "He may be a stallion, but he walks away from his herd to see you. I love it when he puts his head over your shoulder, as if you're another horse." She pauses, then takes a deep breath. "But Blue is wild and he loves to run. Perhaps you should go and run a bit too?"

"But Mom's back in Idaho," I whisper, thinking of her grave on the hilltop where the wild grasses grow. When I'm home, I visit her almost every day.

"Oh, Jenna, honey." Barb gives me a hug. "Your mom would want you and your dad to be happy again. It's been three years now, and time you got on with your life. Have some adventures of your own, especially while Greg and Maggie are off traveling in New Zealand."

"I hate to admit it, but I'm scared. Afraid to leave you guys and Blue."

"Life is scary, Jenn, but remember when you first rode Blue? The exhilaration of doing something out of your comfort zone? And look how much happiness he has brought you."

I smile. "You're right, of course. Maybe I could just go away for a little bit?"

"It's just a plane ride." Doug's practicality calms me down. "If you don't like being away, you can jump on another plane and come right home. Go have some fun."

I look down at Maggie's keys and think of Dan, of his church Nativity at Christmas, of the crisp cold and his warm arms. "Maybe I could go to England? Perhaps on the same flight as Dan?"

As I say the words, Dan walks along the path toward the restaurant, his handsome face turned up to catch his last rays of San Diego sun. He comes in and heads toward us.

Barb smiles. "Why don't you ask him?"

Chapter 3

"Ask me what?" Dan arrives at our table, his leather laptop bag swinging from one shoulder. "Whatever the question is, the answer's yes."

He looks down at me. I take a deep breath and hold the keys out to show him. I plunge in before I lose my nerve.

"Maggie gave me these and I've never been to England before. Could I go to the airport with you and maybe even take the same plane? What do you think?"

My words tumble over each other but Dan smiles as he bends to look more closely at the keys.

"Wow, lucky you! Maggie's cottage is cool. None of my family have keys, only Sam and Harry. And of course you can come on the shuttle with me. There are lots of flights to London. Have you checked to see if you can get a ticket?"

"Not yet, but I've got my passport with me and a travel credit card from Dad. Could I get a ticket at the airport?"

"Let's try." Dan looks at his watch. "Same-day international tickets are difficult, so we'll see what's available when we get there. I'll wait at Reception while you get your things, but hurry now, the shuttle leaves in twenty minutes."

I can't hide my huge grin as I hug Doug and Barb. "I'll text you to let you know what's happening. Could you find Susan and the girls so I can say goodbye on my way out?"

They nod as I run upstairs to grab my bag. I'm going to England – with Dan Martin!

I hug myself with excitement and throw things into my backpack. I don't have much with me and to be honest, my wardrobe consists mainly of faded denim. I'm downstairs again in fourteen minutes to hug Susan and the girls before Dan and I board the airport shuttle.

As it pulls away, I wave out of the back window and I'm suddenly aware of what I'm doing. Is this crazy?

I could get off right now. I could stay.

"Are you okay?" Dan's warm hazel eyes are concerned.

I take a deep breath. "I guess so. Thanks for your help."

He takes my hand. "I'm happy to have more time with you, Jenna."

At the airport, I head for the ticketing desk while Dan gets us coffee. I ask the agent if I there's room on the same flight as his.

"Only in First Class, ma'am."

I remember that Dad paid for everyone to fly First Class to the wedding, so that's where Dan will be. "Yes, please, a First Class ticket to London Heathrow."

It sounds great, just saying it out loud. With that taken care of, I join Dan for coffee before we go through Security into the Departures lounge. We pass a tourist shop and I see a cuddly toy, a soft brown bear in a cute, striped t-shirt with San Diego written on the front. I pick it up and stroke the soft fur. For a moment, I long to buy it for something to hold onto. But no, it would be a babyish thing to do, and Dan would think I'm silly.

I browse magazines to read on the flight and lose Dan for a minute. When we meet again outside the shop, he's holding something behind his back.

He grins as he gives me the little bear. "I thought you might like something to remember this trip."

I cuddle it close. "Thank you. That's so thoughtful."

"You're setting out on a big adventure, Jenna. You need a traveling companion."

"Then I'll call him Dan."

He laughs and gives me a hug. For a moment, I think he might kiss me, but then our flight is announced on the airport intercom.

"Let's go."

We arrive at the gate, and Dan waves me forward. "You can board now, Jenna. You're in First Class."

"But, I thought you were too? Dad said everyone was coming First Class to the wedding?"

"It's a long story. I'll tell you another time. But you won't miss being in Economy, that's for sure. Have a good flight and I'll see you at the other end."

I'm confused, but the excitement of the flight overtakes me. I walk onto the plane, welcomed to my seat by a friendly attendant with a glass of champagne. I wish Dan were here beside me, but I'm going to make the most of this trip anyway.

First Class is excellent. Once the plane takes off, I choose a delicious *a la carte* meal, served on china plates with real silverware. It's a completely different experience from flying Boise to San Diego, when I had a cold chicken wrap covered in foil.

The sleeping couch is roomy, and if I turn slightly onto one side, it's just long enough for my legs. I'm able to sleep comfortably with linen sheets under a soft, warm blanket. I put in earplugs, cuddle around Dan, my little bear, and fall asleep to the distant roar of the engines.

It seems like only minutes before I'm woken for breakfast. I freshen up in the spacious restroom and sit close to the window as the plane descends in slow spirals over London.

I've always wanted to visit. Susan and Todd came as children with Mom and Dad. I thought that one day I would arrive in the city with him, but I'm here alone, and although I keep thinking of Dan in Economy, I don't want to be dependent on him. Perhaps I should even spend my first night in London on my own?

The Captain's voice comes over the intercom, informing us of the local time and I adjust my watch. "Thank you for flying with us today. We wish you a safe onward journey and happy holidays."

I look out of the window again. The clouds part to reveal an ancient city. It's sprawled and wandering, not planned like on a neat US grid system. To the west, I can see a huge reservoir with green fields where sheep and horses graze. Below me, the great River Thames winds through the city toward the sea. I'm excited about exploring London, and I wish Dan were beside me as we come in to land.

I don't see him in the Passport line, as British nationals go through electronic passport gates. Eventually, I make it to Baggage Claim. My heart skips a beat as I see him waiting with both our bags at his feet. He looks up as I approach and his smile lights up his face.

"How was your flight?"

"Amazing. I slept so well and the food was great. So, tell me, why weren't you in First Class?"

He dodges the question. "I'm just glad we're both here safely." He picks up the bags. "I've spoken to Mum, and she says it's okay for me to bring a friend for Christmas. Would you like to come and stay in Summerfield?" His voice is hesitant. "You can always go to Maggie's cottage, but I thought you might like some company on your first visit to England, especially as it's Christmas?"

"I'd love to stay with you and your family. I'm keen to see your Nativity play as well." I look down at my backpack, aware that I don't have anything decent to wear. I don't think my jeans will be appropriate for a British Christmas Day. "But I'd like to do some shopping first."

Dan nods. "That suits me. I've arranged to meet

an Australian friend tonight to go over my travel plans for after Christmas."

His words send a chill through me. In my excitement, I'd forgotten that Dan is leaving again so soon for the other side of the world. But at least we'll have some time together before then.

We exit into the Arrivals area and Dan helps me get some pounds, British currency, out of the ATM. The notes are strange and I can't figure out the exchange rate. It's all so foreign. I suddenly feel a long way from the ranch, but there is a place that Dad considers a second home in London. I put a hand on Dan's arm.

"My dad always stays at the Dorchester. Do you think I could go there tonight while you're with your friend?"

Dan's eyes widen slightly. "Nice place. Let's get you a cab." He escorts me to the taxi rank and helps me with my bag. He leans in to kiss my cheek. "Enjoy yourself. I'll come and get you at the Dorchester tomorrow at 3 p.m."

"See you tomorrow."

As the taxi pulls away, I have a moment of panic. Dan's gone. I'm on my own in London, one of the biggest cities in the world. We're driving on what feels like the wrong side of the freeway. Heavy rain hammers on the roof, obscuring the view. It's cold and I shiver, pulling my old coat around me, the familiar smell of the ranch already fading. What am I doing here?

I gaze out the window, pushing aside my anxiety. I can't run home as soon as I've arrived.

Soon we're driving down one side of a park and then the taxi pulls into the Dorchester Hotel. It's incredibly grand, and for a moment, I don't want to get out. I've never been anywhere like this before.

"Forty-two pounds, please." The driver's voice breaks into my thoughts. I add a twenty-percent tip and wish him happy holidays.

A doorman in a dark green and gold uniform with a black top hat opens the taxi door. He holds an umbrella and shelters me from the rain as I emerge. He looks surprised at my bedraggled state and his nose wrinkles at the smell of my old coat.

"Welcome to the Dorchester." I smile and start up the front steps, but he puts a white-gloved hand out to stop me. "I'm sorry miss. I think perhaps you're at the wrong entrance? If you're here for the position of Housemaid, the staff entrance is around the side. Our guests will complain if you go through the front entrance dressed like that."

Chapter 4

I blush scarlet and look down at my tatty coat – my only coat, except for the sheepskin I wear on the ranch. My black jeans and comfortable boots look okay, but I guess my hair is greasy, tied up in a knot on top of my head. My old backpack bulges with what little I have with me.

"I look like a housemaid?" The doorman looks surprised to hear my American accent.

At that moment, a dark blue Rolls-Royce pulls up, a chauffeur in an official uniform visible in the front. The doorman ushers me gently to one side and steps forward to open the door.

"Good afternoon, Your Excellency."

He stands to attention as a tall man steps out of the limo, wearing the long white robes of the Middle East. He's followed by two beautiful women in elegant coats and high heels. They don't even glance at me.

As soon as they're inside, the doorman indicates we should step behind a bank of potted plants. His smile is friendly. "Now, young lady, how may I help you?"

I feel vulnerable and out of place but he looks kind, so I take a deep breath and try to explain. "My name's Jenna Warren. My father is Greg Warren, an American oil executive who often stays at the Dorchester. He's in New Zealand right now. I've just flown in on my first visit to London and didn't know where to go, so I thought …"

The doorman nods. "Of course, I remember Mr. Warren. Please excuse me for suggesting you might be here for a job. Under the circumstances, I still think that Mrs. Hudson, our Head of Housekeeping, will be the best person to help you. Let me call her."

He moves away to use a hotel phone and I slump against the wall with fatigue. He comes back after a minute or two.

"Mrs. Hudson will be down shortly, Miss Warren. Come this way and I'll find someone to take you to her. Don't worry now, we'll look after you."

We walk around the side of the hotel and stand to one side as a delivery truck roars up the service ramp. The doorman rings the bell next to an inconspicuous gray door. It's opened by a petite Asian woman wearing a crisp Dorchester uniform, her hair neatly tied back.

"This is Miss Warren. I think she could use a cup of coffee while she waits for Mrs. Hudson." The doorman grins and puts his hand up, speaking in a stage whisper behind it. "We can't talk about it, but I hear she's just returned from making an American reality TV show, like *Survivor*." He touches his top hat and turns to go.

"Thanks so much for your help."

"You're welcome, Miss Warren."

"Please come in." The young woman smiles and leads me down a corridor painted a clean light green. We go into an empty room with chairs, functional tables and a coffee station. She helps me to coffee and cream, then excuses herself.

"Mrs. Hudson will be along shortly."

I sip coffee and stare around me, feeling desperately out of place in the basement of the Dorchester Hotel. This is not how I expected to arrive in England.

The door opens, and a woman in her fifties enters, dressed in a smartly tailored suit. Her hair is a fashionable dark blonde bob, and she wears a discreet Dorchester name badge. *Mrs. Jane Hudson, Head of Housekeeping.* She carries a clipboard and a small wallet used for key cards. She looks me up and down and then her stern face breaks into a smile.

"Hello, Jenna. I recognize you. Your father has shown me pictures of you over the years." Relief floods through me and suddenly, I know everything will be okay. "Our doorman says that you've just come back from filming a reality TV show and need a place to rest and recover?"

I laugh. "Either that or I need a job as a housemaid. I think he was being kind and trying to cover for my appearance. My dad's on his honeymoon in New Zealand, but I know he stays here. It's my first trip to England and I wanted to see the Dorchester."

"Of course. We didn't know that Mr. Warren had recently re-married. I'll personally make sure that our signature champagne will be on ice for his next visit. Please come this way. I'll take you up to your room immediately."

We go back along the corridor to the service elevator. As we slowly ascend, Mrs. Hudson turns to me, "Would you like some shopping recommendations or help from a personal stylist? We have a wonderful spa and beauty salon. You can have treatments or a hair appointment. What can we do to make this visit memorable for you?"

Her warm brown eyes remind me of Barb, so I just blurt it out. "To be honest, this is my first trip away from home. I live on the ranch and work with horses, so this is all a little strange. I see how stylish everyone is and – " I hesitate to tell her, but why not? I have nothing to lose. "There's someone coming to get me tomorrow and I'd like to look as good as possible. Can you help me?"

Mrs. Hudson smiles. "If there's someone special coming tomorrow, then perhaps a complete make-over is needed. I'll call our spa for you."

The elevator stops at the fourth floor and we step out into a wide corridor. The walls are pale apricot and the doors a darker shade. There are huge vases of fresh flowers, different varieties but all a creamy magnolia color. Their delicate perfume fills the air as Mrs. Hudson opens the door to a fabulous room.

"I'll let you freshen up. I can recommend the room service menu, if you're hungry."

I carefully place my backpack by the door, aware of how dirty it is. The room is decorated in pale cappuccino and looks out over the park. It has a king-size bed with a beautiful coffee and cream bedspread, piled high with elegant pillows.

"It's beautiful, thank you."

Mrs. Hudson looks down at my backpack. "We have arrangements with several boutiques on Bond Street. They bring their fashions in-house for special clients. I can arrange that if you wish."

Time to use that credit card again.

I smile at her. "That would help. Maybe then I can ride in the main elevator and walk across the lobby with the other guests?"

"Certainly." Mrs. Hudson laughs gently. "Once you've had a Dorchester makeover, you'll be able to step out anywhere in this city."

"Thank you. Then I'll order some food and take a shower."

"I'll speak with Isabelle in the spa and ask her to contact you later this evening." Mrs. Hudson walks to the door, looking back at me as she leaves. "Welcome to the Dorchester, Miss Warren."

* * *

The next morning, I'm up early for a series of appointments in the spa and beauty salon. I flick through European magazines as I'm having my hair cut and styled, looking at images of celebrity women in gorgeous clothes. I feel so far away from the ranch and Blue, but this is exciting. I've never been a girly girl, but who wouldn't feel special in this luxury?

I have a manicure and a light make-over. Nothing too dramatic, but it's enough to make me look quite different. My cheekbones stand out with a touch of blush and for the first time, I truly see my Grandmother's Native American beauty shining through.

Isabelle, the stylist, is French and I can't get enough of her accent. She's willowy with ash-blond hair and is almost as tall as I am. She chooses a selection of clothes for me to try on. First, some fitted designer jeans with a jacket that Isabelle says is casual. I can't think of an event in Boise where I'd wear it again, but it's stunning and I feel great.

Then I try on a simple black dress that makes me look – dare I even think it – sophisticated?

Isabelle appraises me as I turn in front of the mirror. "Walk tall and beautiful, Jenna. I know our height is a challenge and it's tempting to hunch over. But people are attracted to vitality." She strokes down the length of my hair, hanging loose around my shoulders. "Be proud of your fabulous raven hair, your expressive eyes." She grins. "And those long, long legs. Make the most of them, and smile. You have a strong face, and it lights with infectious joy when you smile. Turn that on, and your friend will be, how you say, eating out of your hand?"

I straighten my spine and walk tall, glancing over my shoulder at the stylish young woman in the mirror. For a moment, I see what Isabelle sees, then the facade falls away, and my face crumples.

"It's an act, Isabelle. This isn't really me."

"Jenna, ma chèrie." Isabelle shakes her head at me. "The world is a stage, and we are the players, as Shakespeare said. For most people, confidence is an act and there's nothing wrong with that. So, turn it on for me. Pretend and have fun."

I giggle and then stalk across the room with my new, faked confidence.

"Magnifique!" Isabelle applauds, and then looks at her watch. "It's almost three o'clock and time to meet your friend. I'm going to be watching at the window, so walk tall. Don't let me down."

I change into the black fitted jeans, a fine cashmere sweater and tall leather boots. Isabelle carefully brushes my hair and holds the elegant black coat for me so I can slip my arms into the sleeves. I turn and clasp her hands. "Thank you so much, Isabelle. I've learned such a lot today."

"I had as much fun as you, Jenna. I hope to see you again, next time you stay at the Dorchester."

I settle the account from my room and walk tall along the corridor to the elevator. Heads turn as I glide across the lobby, a footman following with my black leather luggage. I try to channel Audrey Hepburn. In my fitted coat, high black boots and stylish dark glasses, I swing a matching designer purse on a strap over my shoulder.

The same friendly doorman touches his top hat as I approach. "Good afternoon Miss Warren." He holds the door wide for me and gives a tiny smile as he bows.

"Good afternoon." I smile from behind my shades, as I sweep graciously to the top of the steps. As I pass close to him, I whisper, "Thank you."

The front entrance area is busy, but I see Dan leaning against a fiery-red Range Rover, scanning the faces of people around him.

A wave of anxiety suddenly rises. What if he doesn't like this new me? What if this is all for nothing?

Chapter 5

Dan looks relaxed and handsome in blue jeans and a tan roll-neck sweater, his arms casually folded across his chest. He watches as I gracefully descend the front steps and his eyes linger with appreciation. But I don't see recognition there.

I hear Isabelle's voice in my head. *Chin up, shoulders back. Walk like a princess.* The glossy raven's wing of my hair swings in its perfect cut. From behind the dark glasses, I see Dan's eyes narrow as he looks at me more closely. His mouth drops open slightly as I walk up to him and angle the sunglasses down my nose a little. I smile over them.

"Whoa, Jenna!" Dan grins, his eyes shining. "You look stunning!"

I spin around, flaring out my coat and hair. "Cool, huh?"

He nods emphatically. "And some. How did you manage that transformation?"

"Ah, Dorchester secrets."

Dan takes my hands, and I hope Isabelle can see us from the window of the spa. Electricity flickers between us as he leans in and kisses my cheek.

"You look beautiful. I'll have to fight off all the men at the party tonight." He smiles broadly as he loads my bag into the back of the Range Rover. "Remember I told you I once had a dressage horse? Well, when I brought him in from the field, he was classy underneath, but covered in mud. When he was cleaned up and polished, wearing all his show tack, he looked like a million dollars."

I tilt my head to one side. "And where exactly are you going with this comparison?"

"In your show tack, with your hair so beautifully cut, you look like Royal Connection about to go into the ring."

I widen my eyes in mock horror. "Dan Martin! Are you comparing me to your dressage horse?"

We laugh together and I think of Blue and how much I love horses, so I appreciate his comparison. Dan opens the front passenger door, and offers his hand to help me in.

We're soon in the London traffic, on the way to

an English family Christmas. I love that he's driving me. "Is this your car?"

Dan shakes his head. "No, it's Mum's pride and joy. I couldn't afford this on a teacher's salary. Mine is an old Jeep with roof bars for my mountain bike. I'm wearing it into the ground before I go to Australia ..."

His words trail off and I realize again how short our time will be together. It's not long before he leaves for Australia, so I must make the most of what we have.

We drive along the freeway and out into the countryside, passing villages and patchwork fields with black and white cows. Dan explains that they're Friesians, dairy cattle. We talk about farming in England and Idaho, and the time flies by. It's not long before we turn into a narrow village street with a sign for Summerfield.

There are old stone cottages on either side as we drive through, some with straw-thatched roofs. Lights shine from the windows, making them look like a picture from a traditional English Christmas card.

Dan pulls up outside a high gate at the end of a lane with an engraved sign, *Home Farm*. He presses the electronic opener above the sunshield and the gate slides open smoothly, closing behind us after we drive in.

The farmhouse is long and low, built of warm red brick, and latticed with black beams. Light blazes from every downstairs window and I can see people inside, holding wine glasses. It looks like the party has already begun. A tingle of apprehension ripples down my spine. What will these people think of me?

"What a beautiful house!" I hide my concern. Might as well try Isabelle's recommendation of faking confidence.

"Thank you." Dan drives the Range Rover into a triple garage and switches off the engine. "It's about four hundred years old. Granddad Arthur bought it for Mum when I was born. Lizzie and I have been so lucky growing up here. Let's get inside. It's cold out here."

He takes my luggage from the car and we walk together across the graveled front yard. I look up at the imposing house. A flight of old stone steps leads to a massive studded front door. There's a horse-head door knocker encircled by a wreath of dark green holly leaves with wide gold ribbons. A stone lion sits by the door, one paw raised, as if on guard duty.

We reach the foot of the steps just as the door

is flung open. Dan's mom, Christine, stands silhouetted against the light, wearing immaculately tailored English riding clothes. She peers out into the dark, shading her eyes with her hand.

"Daniel, darling. What kept you? You know I wanted you to greet our guests."

We climb the steps and walk into the light. Christine narrows her eyes, glaring at me with undisguised hostility. "Who's this?"

I'm a little startled. It's not quite the welcome I was expecting.

"It's Jenna." Dan gives her a quick hug and she clings to him. "Remember, Greg's daughter from the wedding? I rang you from the airport. You said I could bring a friend, so Jenna's staying with us over Christmas."

"I thought you meant Harry." Christine stares at me, stony-faced. "You don't look like the girl from the wedding."

"I had a makeover in London." My voice is soft and apologetic. I want to turn and run away from her anger. I don't know what I've done. But Dan seems oblivious to his mother's cold behavior and steps past her into the hallway.

"Come in, Jenna."

Christine blocks my way, but then Lizzie walks into the hallway.

"Jenna, how wonderful to see you again! You look amazing." She takes my hand, drawing me into the warm. Christine wrinkles her nose as I pass as if I smell bad. I'm glad I'm not wearing my old coat.

"Hello, Mouse." Dan kisses his sister on the cheek, rolling his eyes as he turns away from his mom.

Lizzie is enthusiastic in her welcome. "There are lots of people here for drinks and nibbles before we walk to the church for Dan's class Nativity performance. It's great to see you. I love your hair like that."

"We don't have any guest rooms free." Christine still stands by the open door, her voice as frosty as the air outside. "I thought Harry was coming and he usually stays in the studio with you, Daniel. You *said* you were bringing Harry."

Lizzie smiles warmly at me. "It's okay, Mum, Jenna can stay in my room."

Dan gives his sister a hug. "Thanks. Come on, Jenna."

Christine shrugs her shoulders and closes the front door. "I suppose that will work. Maggie said you like horses. If you're staying, you'd better come and meet the ponies." She sounds slightly more friendly and stares down at my expensive leather boots. "There's old gear in the boot room."

Behind her mother's back, Lizzie nods vigorously,

encouraging me to go. It seems like Christine is trying to recover from a bad start and at least we have horses in common. So how bad can she really be?

"Thanks, I'd like that."

"I'm feeding them in the next ten minutes. Come and find me."

Lizzie hangs my coat in a closet as Dan opens the door to the sitting room. A wave of warmth and laughter rolls out with the buzz of people talking, the clink of wine glasses and the fragrant smell of pine logs. Comfortable, upholstered armchairs and couches are placed around a big log fire that burns brightly, crackling in the hearth. A tastefully decorated Christmas tree touches the ceiling with its Christmas star. Two waiters in black, with floor-length white aprons, carry trays of finger food around as the bar staff serve drinks.

"Dan!" A young man calls from the opposite side of the room. "Come and talk to us, and bring your friend."

"In a minute, guys." Dan turns to me. "Glass of bubbles, Jenna? Lizzie?"

"Yes, please." It might just be Christmas after all.

Lizzie shakes her head. "Not for me, Dan, I'm supervising in the kitchen. I'll have one with you later."

Dan takes two champagne flutes from a passing

waiter and we clink glasses. He leans close, his eyes fixed on mine. "Welcome to Summerfield, Jenna, and Happy Christmas." We sip and I'm feeling better by the minute. "I'm sorry Mum was confused. I obviously wasn't clear enough when I called."

"I'll go see the ponies with her and everything will be fine."

But apprehension rises within me at the thought of being alone with Christine.

Dan looks at his watch. "Right, let's get you settled. I need to be at church for the last sound check."

He goes ahead with my bags, Lizzie and I following. We climb a magnificent staircase paneled in dark oak and hung with framed paintings of horses. On the landing, Dan opens another door and we go up a second flight of narrow stairs, this time with cream painted walls and no carpet. The servant's quarters, perhaps? Doesn't Lizzie have a room in the main section of this grand house?

Dan puts my bags down by one of two doors. "I've got to run but Lizzie will look after you. See you later."

He gives me a quick peck on the cheek before clattering back downstairs and I'm left alone with Lizzie. I'm suddenly a little uncomfortable. We barely spoke at Dad and Maggie's wedding, and now we're sharing a room.

"Sorry that Mum's a bit stressed." Lizzie pushes open the door to a long room in the roof. It has slanting windows and two single beds. "The caterers didn't deliver what she ordered, so I've had to make mini-pizzas." She looks at her watch. "They're in the oven and I need to rescue them before they burn. Come down as quickly as you can. Mum will make up the feeds, then she'll bring in the mares. She's at her most relaxed with the ponies, so it's good you'll get a chance to talk with her."

Lizzie pats the narrow bed nearest the window. "This one's yours. I sleep near the door, so I can get out early in the morning. Sorry that it's a bit primitive up here. The bathroom's next door."

"It's fine. Thanks so much for letting me stay."

Lizzie heads back downstairs, closing the door behind her. Under the glare of overhead neon lighting, her room is plain with a thin carpet and tired-looking bedspreads. The only personal things are art materials on the big table, some shelves of books and stuffed animals on her bed.

I open my black bag and unzip the Dorchester garment protector, unwrapping the tissue to reveal the black cocktail dress. It looks way too sophisticated but I hang it in the closet anyway so that any creases will smooth out. I put my little bear on the pillow and leave the rest of the unpacking for later.

I slip a quilted jacket on over my sweater and go back downstairs.

Lizzie shows me the boot room and I pull on thick socks and a long raincoat. I swap black leather for green gumboots, and she hands me a big travel mug of coffee as we step outside into the cold. The security lights come on as Christine stalks over.

"Coffee, Mum?" Lizzie asks, but Christine either doesn't hear or chooses not to answer.

We walk through the yard behind the farmhouse. It's dark and cold, and I'm grateful for the hot coffee. Two black Labradors appear, greeting us with wriggling bodies and wagging tails. I bend to fondle their silky ears.

"This is Pluto." Christine strokes the older dog. "That's his idiot son, Jester. He eats anything and everything, including leather boots, so watch out for yours."

Accompanied by the dogs, we walk through an orchard and pick some late eating apples. Pockets bulging, we walk to the top of the yard, where a bunch of ponies jostle each other at the gate.

"The Welsh Mountain breed is ideal for children's ponies. Now then, best manners, line up please."

To my astonishment, the mares get into a line, like kids in a schoolyard. With a monologue of comments, Christine checks each one. She runs an experienced hand over their backs and bends to examine their hooves. She clearly loves them and I warm to her a little more as she becomes totally absorbed, just as I do with our horses at home.

"This is Winnie, herd matriarch." Christine lets the mare into the yard, followed by a little wooly sheep. "That's Clive, her companion. He came under the fence one day, and he's been with her ever since."

Christine gives a small sweet apple to each and indicates that I should feed one to the next mare in line. I feel like an awkward kid, but I love the familiar feel of a soft muzzle against my palm. There are eight pony mares, and as the last one comes through the gate, I say quietly, "I miss Blue, my Appaloosa stallion. I've had him for ten years, since he was foaled."

Christine closes the gate, and we walk toward the barn. I try to engage her again, attempting to build a bridge from these fragile beginnings. "Dan told me he had a fabulous horse once, and won prizes for dressage."

Christine stops and spins on her heel. Her eyes are blazing, her teeth bared like a rabid dog. Her bright red hair is lit by the security lights behind her, a nimbus of flame around her head. She steps closer, trapping me against the side of the barn.

"Is that why you've come here?" She spits slurred words right in my face. "Think you're taking my Daniel home as some kind of prize, do you? Well, think again."

Chapter 6

I shrink back. "No, no. Of course not."

Christine glares at me and strides off toward the barn. I'm left standing in the dark, frozen by her anger. How I can face her again after that?

But the cold seeps through my coat, and I can't stand out here forever. The kitchen windows are brightly lit, and I see Lizzie bustling about inside, blonde hair tied back, an easy smile for those working around her. It looks like a refuge.

I sneak into the boot room and change, then carry my empty coffee mug to the kitchen. Lizzie turns with a smile, and then sees the look on my face.

"Jenna, whatever happened?" Her smile falls. "Was Mum difficult?"

I sit on one of the high stools at the counter.

"She was like two different people," I say quietly, so only Lizzie can hear. "One minute she was friendly, showing me the ponies, the next she looked as if she wanted to kill me. I don't know what to do."

"I'm so sorry." Lizzie puts a hand on my arm. "Dan seems quite into you, so she must be feeling threatened."

I shake my head. "But we're not in any kind of relationship. Nothing's happened between us."

Yet.

I remember his face in the moonlight on the beach in San Diego, his gentle kiss and look of admiration at the Dorchester. I want more, but it seems like anything other than a flirtation with Dan Martin would be complicated.

Lizzie sighs. "Dan is Mum's favorite. She's desperately upset about him going to Australia. Of course, we're used to Mum's mood swings, but we try to keep them from our friends. Dan will be mortified when we tell him."

"Then let's not tell him."

Lizzie smiles, just as the oven pings. "Agreed. Do you fancy a hot mini-pizza? You must be ravenous."

She opens the oven door, and a delicious smell wafts out. Lizzie arranges pizzas on dishes, saving two for us. Servers take them into the party, while we sit together at the breakfast bar. I bite through a perfect crust into spicy tomato, onions, oregano and melting cheese. It's delicious, and exactly what I need.

"Did you make these yourself?"

Lizzie nods, blushing a little. "I love to cook, and Mum hates the kitchen. This is my escape."

Dan arrives in a hurry. "Sorry Jenna, I'm just dashing out to the church again. The donkey is acting up. Can't have Mary walking to the manger now, can we? Would you mind coming along later with Liz?"

My mouth is full of pizza, so I nod. "Umm-hmm."

Dan grins. "Glad you're settling in."

If only he could have seen me earlier, cowering in the face of his mother's rage. But perhaps everything will be fine if I can just stay out of her way.

I help Lizzie clear up the kitchen as the sounds of a well-fed crowd filter in from the other room, punctuated by Christine's laugh. I imagine her holding court, the center of attention.

Lizzie switches on the dishwasher. "Right, let's get going. It's a tiny church and we want to get a good seat. Best to be early."

I put on my black designer coat and Lizzie brings out an extravagant Russian fur hat from the closet.

"Here, Jenna, this will keep you warm on the walk."

I put it on and stare in the mirror. A tall, stylish

woman in a designer outfit looks back at me with sparkling dark eyes and gleaming black hair. Not a trace of the cowgirl from Boise.

"I love it! I look like someone out of Dr. Zhivago."

Lizzie pulls on a royal blue coat with toggles and a hood. "You look fantastic. It was a gift from Aunt Viv when she went on a trip to Moscow, but I'm too small for a style like that. I'd love you to keep it."

I give her a hug. "Thanks, Lizzie. You've made me feel so welcome."

She hugs me back and then stuffs her blonde ponytail into a blue woolen hat. "This keeps my glasses in place."

We step out into the cold and our breath frosts in the still air. The Labradors come bounding from the barn to greet us, and we stroke them as they wag their tails happily. "They're in the yard to warn us of strangers," Lizzie says. "There have been thefts of horses around here recently. It would finish Mum if we lost any of the mares."

We walk around the house and across the driveway. The party is still going strong, the wine flows and food is plentiful. Christine stands out with her flame-red hair. She's now wearing a stunning dress of emerald green, looking every inch the fading Hollywood star. Lizzie smiles wistfully as she looks in at her mother.

"Mum's always been a lot of fun. She would take us out of school sometimes just to go on crazy trips to the seaside when the sun was high. Or she'd wake us up with chocolate cake in the middle of the night." Her expression saddens. "But those days are rare now and her anger has become more destructive over the years. When I was younger, I used to climb trees to get away from her and read. I found hiding places so I could draw in peace, because she ridicules my artwork if she finds it. I just try to stay out of trouble now."

We walk down a lane between hedgerows of hawthorn and holly. "What was your mum like? Maggie said she died a few years ago. I'm sorry."

I take a deep breath. "Yes, Mom died of cancer. She was the rock of our family, and there was never a time when I had to hide from her. We used to ride together when she was well and I could tell her anything."

We pass a cottage with a Christmas wreath on the door and the sound of Christmas carols from inside. Our footsteps make imprints in the frost.

"She sounds lovely." Lizzie's voice is wistful. "Mum can be a nightmare, but I had loving grandparents and wonderful aunts." She grins. "And Dan's alright as big brothers go, so I've been lucky there too. I try to understand that Mum is just different. Grandma said that as a baby, she rarely laughed or cried. They got special teachers for her, and as she grew up, she related to people better. Mum was reading at age two, had her first piano lessons when she was three, and has always been good with animals. Grandpa told Dan and me that we're all created differently. He used to say, 'She's our Christine, and we accept her just as she is.'"

Church bells ring out across Summerfield, calling the village to worship. Lizzie gazes up at a dark sky with faint twinkling stars. "On such a night," she says softly, "a King was born in Bethlehem."

As we walk between the country cottages, we soon find ourselves mingling with others heading toward St Peter's Church. Children run about, bundled up in warm clothes, shouting with excitement.

We enter the ancient graveyard and walk along a path between headstones leaning at odd angles. The stone church tower looms above us as Lizzie guides me to an open door and we enter the choir area. It's as cold inside as out, but it seems appropriate as the interior has been transformed into a stable, with bales of hay and a manger.

A little stage is set in front of the altar, and next to it, a beautiful Christmas tree. Colored lights glow in dark green branches and the smell of pine needles fills the air. I follow Lizzie into a row of seats next to the stone effigies of a knight and his lady, a little stone dog curled at their feet. At the main door, a minister in black with a white robe greets the villagers of Summerfield. To one side, a small group of musicians tune their instruments.

I look around for Dan. He's on the other side of the church, marshaling young shepherds into line, each holding a wooly toy lamb. One drags his through the dust by the tail. Dan must sense my gaze, because he turns and smiles. He's wearing a brown shepherd's smock over his jeans, but even with that rustic simplicity, he looks handsome and responsible. I'd trust kids with him.

Gradually, the church fills with families and Christine arrives with her party. Everyone stands as the minister welcomes us. At a signal from Dan, two rows of angels stand up in the choir. They wear long white robes with gorgeous, up-swept wings of curled white paper.

"I helped the mums make those," Lizzie whispers. "They took hours!"

The organ peals and we sing *O, Come All Ye Faithful*. It's strange to be singing in this ancient English church. I remember singing this carol with Mom years ago, in our church in Boise. I miss her so much, but I know she's smiling down on me now. I look over at Dan singing and wonder what she would think of him. I think she would approve.

The Holy Family come down the aisle, Joseph leading a small brown donkey with Mary sitting side-saddle, cradling her precious baby. The children are concentrating on their parts. The click of cameras from proud parents fills the air as Joseph carefully helps Mary down. A small shepherd leads the donkey out of the side door, her part in the story ended.

The pageant unfolds, a story retold across the Christian world at this time of year. My heart swells at the beauty of the children's faces, and I miss my family, especially Dad and Blue. I see their dear faces in my mind and send a silent prayer for them all to be well. I look over at Dan, hope rising in me. I won't be home for Christmas, but this year, I won't be alone.

Chapter 7

At the end of the service, the angels collect money in colorful plastic buckets for a homeless charity. We leave the church with everyone praising the wonderful atmosphere created by the children. People stand in groups under the crisp night sky, chatting and wishing each other Happy Christmas as they munch mince pies.

Dan is surrounded by his class, who are jumping around and doing high-fives. He congratulates them all on a job well done and our eyes meet over their heads. His gaze is intense, and I blush. When all the youngsters have been picked up, Dan escapes and comes over to where I stand with Lizzie.

"What did you think?"

"Awesome. It was a lovely service and such a well-behaved donkey!"

Dan laughs and turns to his sister. "Did you think it improved from the last rehearsal?"

"Unbelievable difference." Lizzie takes his arm. "And the kids loved doing it, even after all that complaining about the Nativity not being cool. Are you walking home with us?"

"I just need to gather my stuff. If you can wait a few minutes, I can walk back with you." He looks directly at me, but as I open my mouth to say an emphatic 'yes,' I see Christine stalking toward us. I don't think I can bear another encounter, especially not in public.

"I need to go right now," Lizzie says. "The buffet needs to be ready and the wait staff organized for when Mum's crowd arrives."

I jump at the opportunity to avoid another confrontation. "I'll come and help."

Dan's face falls in disappointment, just as Christine walks up. She pulls him into a hug. "That was marvelous, darling. Come and meet Sebastian, he's been in Hawaii." She turns her head imperiously toward Lizzie. "Aren't you seeing to the food?"

She doesn't even look at me.

"Just going now." Lizzie puts her arm through mine, and we turn to walk back to the farmhouse through the quiet village streets.

"So what's going on? Dan's looking at you in a starry-eyed sort of way."

I take a deep breath and change the subject. "Did you say that Dan and Harry, Maggie's son, both went to college in Edinburgh?"

I notice that Lizzie blushes a little at Harry's name. I remember them dancing together at the wedding, but he seemed to treat her more like a little sister.

"Yes, Harry used to stay with us every summer vacation when we were kids, because Maggie worked full time. He and Dan were best buddies and sometimes they let me tag along. Harry doesn't ride, but he enjoys Dan's studio, where the band comes to practice. Dan plays keyboards and guitar, and his friends from the village bring instruments to jam in there. Harry's a fashion photographer and takes photos of dancers and musicians."

"Sounds like fun." We reach the gate to Home Farm. "Does he come to visit often?"

"No, because he lives in Edinburgh now. He usually only comes to Summerfield to see Dan or Maggie." Lizzie frowns. "But I guess he won't come at all now. Maggie will be away in America and Dan is going to Australia." We go inside, and she hangs up our coats. "To be honest, Jenna, if Maggie and Mum weren't such old friends, I don't think Harry would be welcome anyway. He encouraged Dan to stand up to Mum when she wanted him to ride Royal to Olympic level in dressage. He was certainly good enough back then. But it was her dream, not his. He always wanted to be a teacher." A faint grimace of pain twists her face and is swiftly gone again. "It was awful here after he left. One of the few times that Dan fell from grace. But it wasn't for long. He walks on water, as far as Mum's concerned."

I hear a touch of bitterness in her voice, but it's understandable seeing how she's treated. "Does Dan work with the ponies when he's here?"

"Sometimes. We have part-time staff, but I do most of the work. Mum tires quickly nowadays."

There's a knock at the front door and three servers arrive, back from their break. Lizzie greets them and herds them toward the kitchen.

"Mum and her guests will stop at the pub for a drink on the way home and be here in about thirty minutes." Lizzie turns back to me. "I'm so sorry you had a run-in with Mum, Jenna, but the party tonight should be fun. Why don't you go and change?"

Upstairs, I change into the black cocktail dress from the Dorchester. I want to make Dan's head turn again, so I try to do my hair and makeup as Isabelle taught me. Well, near enough!

The dress looks striking with my Italian leather boots. I add a simple, gold chain necklace and hoop earrings from the Dorchester collection, and smooth down my hair. As I dab on some lip gloss, I wonder whether Dan might kiss me under the mistletoe. I giggle, feeling like a teenager before a first date, even though this will be a party filled with people I don't know … and his mother.

I take a deep breath, remembering Isabelle's words. All the world's a stage. So I will act a part tonight, but anxiety still tugs at me. I'm not comfortable at parties, I'd rather be riding Blue in the hills, but I must find the courage to go into that room if I want to be with Dan.

I lock Lizzie's door behind me, not understanding why she's so careful about security in her own home. Maybe because there are so many new staff here tonight?

Voices, laughter, and the clink of silverware on china come from the sitting room as I walk down the stairs. I turn back into the kitchen and give Lizzie her key. She smiles at me.

"You look gorgeous, Jenna!"

I pull my dress down a bit. "I'm nervous. Do you think this is too much?"

"It looks awesome with those boots. I wish I could get away with an outfit like that." Lizzie pushes her glasses up on her nose, and then takes a bottle of wine from the fridge. "How about a glass of Chardonnay to give you some courage?"

I nod and she pours us each a glass, then looks around like a conspirator. "Let me show you something fun. It might help you get over your nerves."

Lizzie leads me to the back of the kitchen and through another door, revealing narrow stairs that wind up behind the wall.

"These come out on the landing directly opposite my bedroom stairs. They were used for the servants or perhaps for other kinds of nighttime activity." She raises an eyebrow and we giggle as we walk up a few stairs to a little curtain. Lizzie pulls it aside. A tiny window looks down into the sitting room. "Take a look."

Through the fish-eye lens, I can see everything in the sitting room. An older man bends to pick prawns from the buffet. A couple stand in a corner, their body language indicating an argument, and a group of sporty types hold court in the center. Wait staff circulate, collecting plates and glasses.

Then I see Dan standing with Christine near the fireplace. An older man, fashionably bald and wearing a tweed suit, roars with laughter at something he says and nudges Christine. Dan's expression is polite, but he keeps looking around the room and glancing toward the door. Is he looking for me?

"Mum has a lot of parties," Lizzie says, "but I manage the kitchen and agency staff. She gets annoyed if things are not spot on, and I was always going along the corridor to check. So Dan had this window put in for me one time while she was away. I can see what's going on and send food when it's needed. From the other side, it looks like a little gilt-framed mirror, but it's really a one-way observation port, like security officers use in airports."

She draws the curtain and we return to the kitchen. I sip my wine, thinking of Dan in the next room. I want to go in and talk to him, but I'm scared of Christine.

Lizzie opens the oven and pulls out a batch of focaccia, the smell of rosemary and thyme filling the kitchen.

"Yum, that looks amazing."

"It's one of my most popular breads at the market stall every weekend. Now, are you going in there? I'm sure Dan will want to see you."

I finish my glass of wine. "I guess it's now or never." I pause to take a deep breath and before I open the door, I try to channel Isabelle. *Walk tall, Jenna. Fake it until you make it. Pretend … and have fun.*

I enter the room with confidence, intending to cross directly to the fireplace and Dan. But he's not there and I can't see him in the crowd.

I don't want to stand in the doorway like an idiot and I'm swiftly losing my nerve. I stride across the room, walking tall like a Hollywood starlet, long black hair swirling around my shoulders. The bald man who was speaking with Christine and Dan is still there, so I head for him.

He looks up as I approach and I see him take in my long legs and the hint of a cleavage in this dress. I wish it was Dan looking at me that way. Why hasn't he sought me out? He should be by my side.

"Hi there." My American voice sounds strange in this very English room. "I'm Jenna, a friend of Dan's."

"Good evening." The bald man takes my hand and brings it up to his mouth to kiss it. He holds it too long, looking as if he wants to lick me. "How lovely to meet you. I'm Tony, and any friend of Dan's is a friend of mine." His eyes twinkle at me. "Maybe a very good friend?"

I stifle a shudder at his flirtation. I'm young enough to be his daughter! But he keeps hold of my hand and then slides an arm around my shoulder. Before I can move away, the crowd parts and Dan looks over at me, his eyes wide. Behind him, Christine's face mottles with rage. She pushes toward us, with Dan right behind her.

Chapter 8

I escape from Tony's grasp just as Christine arrives. She looks daggers at me and takes his arm, turning him away.

"Tony, darling, come and meet Meg. She's just bought a racehorse." She leads him away, her back ramrod-straight, a clear signal to stay away. Tony looks over his shoulder and blows a kiss. I can't hide my grimace of distaste.

Dan takes my arm and steps close. "I'm sorry that old goat hit on you. For some reason, Mum fancies him. You look amazing, Jenna, just gorgeous." He steers me toward the door. "How about we disappear for a bit? We could get some air and I'll show you my studio."

He takes a bottle of wine from the bar and we

escape. I sigh with relief as the voices fade. "Thanks for rescuing me. Do I need a coat?"

Dan takes my hand. "No, it's just across the yard. My own private space." I can't wait to be alone with him, rather than surrounded by noise and people.

As we walk across the yard, I shiver a little in the cold, my cocktail dress hardly a barrier against the winter wind. Dan wraps an arm around me and pulls me close. He releases me to unlock the door to his studio and I miss him already. But once he turns on the lights, I'm fascinated.

It's clearly Dan's domain and so different from the main house. There's a small hallway and then a room set up as a sound studio. It has a big recording deck, a drum kit in the corner and microphones on stands, next to a pair of amplifiers and a full-size electronic keyboard. A guitar leans on a stand and two big sofas create a welcoming space. Posters of bands cover the walls, hiding the sound-proofing.

It's a musician's bachelor pad with a bedroom, en-suite bathroom, and a tiny kitchen.

"I've spent two years building up this sound studio, bit by bit." Dan sits down at the keyboard, plays some chords and then the start of an Adele song. "One day we'll cut a demo worth sending to the record companies. Until then, I'll just keep playing. But it's a good set-up and I'll miss it when

I go to Australia. I've asked Lizzie if she wants to move in here while I'm gone. She could use a nicer room, that's for sure."

His pure notes fill the air, and I sit down next to him on the bench, leaning in to his warmth. I can feel his muscles move as he plays. He sings a chorus and his voice is remarkable, vibrating through me. Up close, Dan has long, dark eyelashes and laughter lines. His hazel eyes have flecks of gold in the mix of green and brown. My heart beats faster as I sense the chemistry building between us, like it did on the beach in San Diego.

He finishes the song and turns to me, cupping my face in his hands. "You're so beautiful, Jenna. Your eyes change in a moment, from serious and soulful, to sparkling and wicked. You bewitch me." He touches his lips to mine, a soft caress, as if asking for permission. I sigh, and he wraps his arms around me, pulling me against his body as the kiss deepens and I lose myself in him.

The door crashes open.

We spring apart at the sound.

"Get out of here!" Christine hisses as she stalks into the studio. "I knew what you were, as soon as I saw you. How dare you come into my house and seduce my son?"

She darts toward me, her hand raised as if to slap

me. Dan jumps up and stands between us. "Mum, stop! What are you doing? Jenna is my guest."

Christine tries to get around Dan to me, and I shrink back. "You've got more sense, surely, Daniel. She was all over Tony back there."

Her voice is shrill, her face almost as red as her hair and her eyes are wild. I'm afraid of her, but at the same time, I hear Lizzie's voice from earlier. Is she sick? Maybe she can't control this jealousy?

Dan holds her back and I can see that he's devastated. He loves his mother, despite her behavior, and I can't make him choose between us.

"Dan, why don't you take me to Square Cottage?"

My calm words break through Christine's rage. "What does she mean?" she demands sharply. "How can she go to Maggie's cottage? I don't even have keys and we've been friends for years." She narrows her eyes at me. "You must have stolen them."

Dan sighs. "Maggie gave the keys to Jenna, Mum. Remember, Maggie married Greg, Jenna's father, so Jenna is part of her family now. She has keys, just like Harry and Samantha."

Christine stalks back toward the door. "Then Maggie's a fool. I heard what happened in Idaho. Daddy's little princess, spoiled rotten. Maggie will regret having her in the family."

Her words are like blows and tears spring to my

eyes. I deeply regret what I did to Maggie, but nothing I say will change Christine's mind. I put a hand on Dan's arm. "Can you drive me there now, please, Dan?"

Christine smiles in triumph, and her voice changes to molasses and sweet cajoling. "You don't need to drive her anywhere, Daniel. Phone for a taxi and come back to the party. You promised you would co-host with me."

For a moment, I think Dan will do what she wants and send me packing, alone into the night. But he takes my hand.

"If Jenna's going, Mum, then I'm going too. You insulted my friend, and I'm ashamed of you."

Christine's face contorts and she begins to cry. "You used to be so good to me, Daniel. You used to be so kind to your mother. What's happened to you?"

I can't keep up with how fast her mood turns, but she's tugging at Dan's heartstrings with years of emotional manipulation. I see him struggle. He wants to support her, and I can't watch this family drama play out anymore. I pull my hand from his.

"Don't worry, Dan. I'll get my things and be on my way."

I slip past Christine, run back to the main house and up to Lizzie's room. Throwing the few things

I'd unpacked into my bag, I struggle to control my tears. I don't want to be alone for Christmas, but here I am, about to be thrown out into the cold.

Chapter 9

There's a crash and a shout. I open Lizzie's window and look down into the yard. Christine is outside the studio, screaming at Dan. He has his arms folded across his chest, his chin raised in defiance.

"If you go with her tonight, Daniel, then don't bother coming back."

I can't help but thrill inside. Dan has chosen me. I pull on my coat, grab my bag, and rush downstairs, ducking out of the side door. Christine has stormed off and Dan is loading a bag into his old Jeep.

He looks up and I see pain in his eyes. "I'm so sorry, Jenna. This isn't turning out to be a great visit. I bet you wish you'd stayed in London."

I take his hand. "I'm happy to be here with you. Is it wrong to think Christmas Eve together, just the two of us, might not be all bad?"

He smiles and bends to kiss me softly. "I think it might be perfect." He sighs. "Things will blow over with Mum in a few days, they always do. She won't speak to me for a bit, and then it will be as if it never happened."

"What about Lizzie? Will she be alright with us gone?"

Dan looks up at the house. "Liz knows exactly how this goes. She's had the sharp end of it for years and has the patience of a saint. I don't know how she puts up with it. Mum's punishing me because I'm off to Australia very soon, but I won't let her ruin my life."

His words run through me like ice. He's leaving so soon for the other side of the world.

"I'll text Lizzie that we're going to Square Cottage. She'll understand."

I think of her with Christine in such a foul mood and worry for her. But Lizzie has clearly developed her own strategies over the years. I don't have such a thick skin.

We drive away from the farmhouse, and I look back. It's probably seen worse things over the years than a few family quarrels.

"We should get groceries," Dan says as we drive out of Summerfield toward the nearest town. "Witney should still be open for last-minute Christmas shoppers. Can't have my guest going hungry."

He drives with confidence through the narrow country lanes, although the hedgerows rising high on both sides make me nervous. It starts to rain and Dan sighs. "I'm so over this winter. San Diego was great for a break, but I'm looking forward to warmth and the sparkling ocean in Australia."

"Where exactly are you going?"

"Cairns in Queensland, on the northeast coast. My dad used to live in Sydney, but he re-married and has a real estate business there now. It's the nearest town to the Great Barrier Reef with a tropical climate and lots of tourism. Lizzie and I have a step-mum, Angelina, whom we've never met, and two little half-brothers and a half-sister."

I can hear in his voice that he's longing to go. And after the run-in with Christine, I can understand his need to escape. But I wish he weren't going so soon.

"What about you, Jenna? Will you go home after Christmas or have some more adventures?"

I stare out of the window into the pouring rain. "Leaving San Diego was such a sudden decision. I guess I don't know what I'm doing next. Maybe I'll go see my brother, Todd. I've been waiting for him to contact me about his plans. There's been some kind of change at the restaurant where he works."

We drive into a market square, still busy although it's dark and getting late. Dan finds a space and somehow squeezes into it. There's a lot less room in England and people park wherever they find a spot. I don't want to drive here, that's for sure.

The booths have colorful Christmas lights and Santa Sleigh decorations flash on and off from the street lamps. Last-minute shoppers hurry by, their bags overflowing with goodies and gifts as they go home after work on Christmas Eve.

Dan leans over and takes my hand. "Enough of the miserable family stuff, Jenna. We didn't plan for this to happen, so let's have some fun and make the best of it. Will you spend this Christmas with me?"

"I'd love to."

Dan puts his arms around me and softly kisses my lips. "Let's buy some delicious food and wine, take it to Square Cottage and celebrate. Just the two of us."

We walk around hand in hand, and the smell of hot food from a bakery hits us as we walk by.

Dan stops. "Hmm, the steak pot pies look good. Are you hungry?"

"Starving."

We eat our pies from white paper bags that are useful hand-warmers in the chilly air. We sit on a bench near the old stone market cross, munching and watching people go by, their faces alight with Christmas cheer.

The houses around the square are built from soft, golden stone. There's a sense of history, of lives played out against the backdrop of hundreds of years. I love America, but I can see why English history draws so many people here.

We finish eating and walk quickly around the booths before everyone closes down. We find a small organic chicken – no turkeys left at this point – vegetables, wine and cheese. Then I find a dear little Christmas tree in a scarlet ceramic pot.

"A bargain at 30% off, plus the bag of trimmings." The stall-holder wraps it for me. "Happy Christmas!"

We head back to Summerfield, away from the lights of the town, and into the darkness of the country.

Dan pulls up in front of a little cottage, a perfect square with a big chimney-pot and smoke curling out of the top. A soft light shines from the downstairs windows and it looks so welcoming. I feel like Snow White finding the cottage of the Seven Dwarfs. Dan brings our bags and the groceries to the front door.

"I texted Selena from the Potlatch that we were coming. She said she'd light the fire."

I look up at the dormant rose stem twisted into the wood over the doorway, imagining it blooming in the summer. "So this is Maggie's Square Cottage. It's beautiful."

"Time to try those new keys, Jenna."

I take the little box from my backpack and unlock the door, opening it directly into the living room. Side lamps cast warm pools of light over a red and blue patterned rug covering half of the big stone tiles. Two comfortable blue couches flank an open fireplace and logs burn cheerfully behind a latticed, metal guard.

There are colorful paintings of flowers on the walls, and a stunning black and white drawing of two hares in a field. Wooden stairs curve upwards opposite the front door, and the little house smells of wood smoke and rose petals. I'm suddenly overwhelmed with gratitude that I have this place as a refuge.

Dan stands behind me, wraps me in his arms and kisses my neck. "Let's get the groceries in and make ourselves at home."

I carry in the little Christmas tree and put it on the window ledge. Dan connects the lights right away and I hang tiny silver bells from its branches. It feels like a celebration.

We unpack the food in the kitchen. There's a knock at the back door, and a petite woman with dark brown hair in a bun stands there, wearing her special Christmas sweater. It's green with a reindeer on the front, the nose glowing rhythmically on and off. She smiles and gives me a little basket of eggs, a carton of milk and what looks like homemade cookies.

Dan smiles and hugs her. "Happy Christmas, Selena. This is Jenna, Greg's daughter."

Selena and I shake hands. "Welcome to Summerfield, Jenna. You look a lot like your dad and I'm so pleased to finally meet you. Have you heard from Maggie and Greg?"

"I had an email from them. They're in the South Island of New Zealand, enjoying the sunshine."

"Good for them. Now let me show you two how to keep warm in Maggie's cottage." Selena turns to a big, black stove: modern but like an old-fashioned range with two shiny silver lids on top, covering circular hotplates. "This is a gas-fired Aga, great for cooking but also for controlling the hot water and central heating. The beds are made up. The towels in the family bathroom upstairs are yours, Jenna. Dan's are in the shower room down here. I need to get back to help Tom now; it's extra busy at the Potlatch on Christmas Eve. Come over later!"

She takes my hands, her eyes crinkling in a smile. "Maggie told me to make you especially welcome. I hope you enjoy your stay at Square Cottage."

Her friendliness is so different from Christine's animosity. "Thank you, Selena."

She leaves and Dan touches the bottle of champagne to his cheek. "This is just cold enough. How about a glass to celebrate?"

"Sounds good."

I find two fluted glasses and Dan pops the cork. We sit on the couch and firelight reflects off his glass as Dan lifts it in a toast.

"Merry Christmas, Jenna."

I touch my glass to his and lean in to gently kiss his lips. "Happy Holidays, Dan."

The bubbles fizz on my tongue, and we gaze into the flames, sipping champagne, at peace with one another. I'm thrilled to be here with him, but I can't help thinking of Lizzie suffering Christine's wrath, then going up to sleep alone in her bare attic bedroom.

"Dan, can I ask you something?"

He puts an arm around me, nuzzling closer. "Anything."

"Why is your mom so hard on Lizzie?"

Dan stares into the flames. "Mum and Dad split up before Lizzie was born. You've seen what she can be like and I don't think he could cope with it anymore. Our grandparents looked after us, along with Mum's sister, Viv. I don't remember much and Lizzie has never met our father …" His voice trails off and he takes a long, reflective sip of champagne. "Dad left for Australia and Mum had a breakdown that lasted until months after Lizzie was born. When she came out of it, she couldn't even remember being pregnant. A combination of post-natal depression and the mood disorder, perhaps, but she rejected the baby. When she's at her most angry, Mum will swear that Lizzie isn't even her daughter."

I shake my head. "That's awful, but Lizzie is your sister, right?"

"Absolutely, we've had paternity tests. But Mum doesn't feel the same way about Lizzie as she does about me. She even blames Lizzie for the break-up of her marriage."

I sigh. "That's so sad."

"Families, the stuff of legend," Dan says. "William Shakespeare lived not far from here. Our greatest English playwright put family drama at the heart of his work. Love and duty, murder and reconciliation." He takes another sip of champagne and looks at me. I see the pain in his eyes. "Enough of that, Jenna. How are you feeling? A little more welcome now, I hope?"

I put my glass down on a side table, wrap my arms around his neck and smile. "Yes, I'm feeling much better."

"Maggie will be pleased that you like Square Cottage. She was worried at the wedding when she asked me to look after you."

I freeze. Then, I look at him, puzzled. "What do you mean, look after me?"

Dan sighs. "Remember you asked why I flew Economy from San Diego to London. I need to tell you, and it might as well be now." He takes a deep breath. "I didn't have enough money for the flight to Cairns, so Maggie exchanged my First Class ticket to the wedding for Economy. I used the balance for my ticket to Australia."

I pull away from him, outraged. "You mean, Maggie *paid* you to babysit me?"

Chapter 10

Dan brushes a strand of hair away from my face and I smack away his hand. "Well, Maggie encouraged me to be friendly and make sure you were safe. Let's face it, you needed some help with that flowerbed."

I can't help but smile. "You did go beyond the call of duty that night."

He leans forward, touching his lips to mine. "This wasn't planned, Jenna. I didn't expect to …"

My heart hammers. I want him to say out loud what I'm feeling, but he kisses me instead. Words are replaced by sensations and I am lost in his arms.

Firelight flickers around us as his strong body presses against mine. He kisses me passionately and I match his kiss. I never want it to end.

But then he pulls away and sits up, face strained.

"Jenna, I want this so much, but I'm leaving soon. I don't want to hurt you. I can't lead you on like this."

"Dan, I –"

He stops me, jumping to his feet and pulling me up after him. "Let's go over to the Potlatch for a Christmas drink. Selena will report us missing to Maggie if we don't, and I wouldn't want to face the wrath of your dad. But let me show you the guest room before we go. I'll be next door in Harry's old room."

I want to stay here, kissing him by the fire, but he's determined. So I follow him up the creaky wooden stairs. The guest bedroom has dusky-pink wallpaper, stenciled with an unusual design of black and white butterflies. There's a comfortable-looking queen-size bed, with the same rose-pink bedspread and pillows.

"It smells of summer."

"It's the dried petals from Maggie's garden. Would you like a shower before we go? I'll bring up our bags."

I take a luxurious hot shower and can't help but imagine his hands on my skin. I turn the water to cold to distract my intimate thoughts. Once finished, I carefully style my hair as Isabelle taught me until my raven mane hangs shining like black silk. I apply light makeup, and dress in black fitted slacks, a black camisole, and an elegant tunic top. I add some of my turquoise and silver jewelry and pull on the designer boots once more. I seem to be living in them, but they are fabulous!

When I go back downstairs, Dan is seated on the couch with his back to me, reading a National Geographic magazine. He's wearing donkey-brown cords and a cream, cable-knit sweater. He looks every inch the country gentleman.

I bend over and kiss him on his smoothly shaven cheek. He smells of coconut shampoo and woody aftershave. "Let's go."

We walk down the drive holding hands and pause at the five-bar gate to look back at our little tree shining in the window.

"To light us home."

Dan leads me the short distance to the pub. The Potlatch Inn is packed with people talking and laughing with Christmas cheer. It's a different crowd from the one gathered at Home Farm with Christine, and I feel more welcome here.

Selena is busy behind the bar and waves as we walk in. Dan introduces me to her Italian husband, Tommaso, known as Tom. "Welcome, Jenna." He kisses me on both cheeks with European flair.

I have a mug of mulled wine, a heady brew of red wine with orange juice and spices. Dan has a pint of local ale and greets some of the neighbors. I lose track of names, but after another mulled wine, I'm happy just to smile.

I'm introduced to Dan's friend, Clair, from the Summerfield Stables.

"Hi Jenna! I met Greg when he came riding with Maggie. Would you like to ride out with us on Boxing Day?"

"I'd love to. Do you have a horse available?"

"Teddy and Tessa, our two sturdy Highlands, are free for you and Dan, if you like." She tells me about Russ, the horse Dad rode and Bella, Maggie's favorite. Soon, we're deep in talk of horses, our mutual passion, and time flies by. Selena calls last orders as the jukebox plays Slade's Merry Christmas one final time.

Dan and I step out into the cold and walk home arm in arm under the stars. The little Christmas tree welcomes us back and we make hot tea in the kitchen and carry it in to the sitting room. Then we sit on the couch together and Dan stirs the logs into flame again. I lean against him in their glow.

"I enjoyed the Potlatch and meeting some of your friends. For the past two Christmases, Dad and I have been with Susan and her family. But now she and Steve are separated, he has the girls for the day with his parents. Susan will be lonely, so I need to call her tomorrow."

"She'll appreciate that." Dan's voice is tired but neither of us wants to go to bed. So we stay and sip our tea, gazing into the fire, as the little Christmas tree lights glow in the window.

"When I was little," I say, softly, "I used to lie under our big family Christmas tree with Mom. We'd pretend we were out in the Payette National Forest, looking up at the stars through the branches. Except, of course, it would have been a bad idea because of mountain lions, bears and wolves."

Dan grins. "What about the Appaloosa horses you mentioned. Aren't they in danger in the forest?"

"They'd only be in there if they were lost or abandoned. They're usually in herds on the grasslands."

Dan wraps his arm around me and gently pulls me close. He tugs a velvet throw from the back of the couch to snuggle around us. "Where does the word Appaloosa come from?"

With a sigh of contentment, I rest my head in the curve of his neck and tell him about home. "The Nimiipuu', which means 'We, the people', are one of the First Nations, and are mostly known as the Nez Perce. They're the largest group living near the Payette Forest and horses have always been their wealth." I turn slightly to get more comfortable, curling around Dan. "They're expert horse breeders. The Palouse River runs through their ancient lands, so their spotted horses were called A-Palouse, and later, Appaloosa. Our ancestors on Dad's side are Native American and I feel especially connected to Appaloosas."

"You said you have an Appaloosa stallion?"

I nod. "Blue, but he's doesn't actually belong to me. He's my Guardian, as I am his. He was foaled ten years ago, from a rescue mare that Barb took in. A big old gray, nothing special to look at, just a mare that needed feeding. We called her Smokey. She bit people a lot, but not me. It turned out that she was in foal."

Dan smiles, leaning back, and the soft light lingers on his face. "Royal Connection used to bite everyone, including me, but never Mum. I think he knew she'd bite him back." He turns to me. "So, Blue was Smokey's foal?"

"Yes." Suddenly, I'm back in a darkened barn with the closed doors rattling in gusts of wind and rain pattering on the roof. Smokey pants as her new foal slips into the world and struggles to stand up.

Dan squeezes my hand. "Are you too tired to talk, Jenna? We can just sit here quietly, if you like."

I come back to the present and squeeze his hand in return. "Sorry. I was just remembering. When Smokey licked the foal dry, his coat shone a pure black with a pattern of white spots on his back and hindquarters. He was the most beautiful leopard-spot Appaloosa, and somehow, there was already wisdom in his eyes. I made a hot mash for Smokey and she let me sit at her feet while he suckled. Then he wandered around, sniffing my clothes and face. After that, he followed me everywhere and I named him Blue, because of his blue-black coat."

"The same color as your beautiful hair. I can tell he means a lot to you. You must miss him."

I think of Blue, galloping across the hills. "I do miss him. He's the spirit horse of an ancient people and mostly wild at heart. Like me, I suppose."

The church bells suddenly ring out, echoing across the village in the chill night air.

It's Christmas Day.

Dan leans in to kiss me. "Happy Christmas, Jenna. I'm so glad to be celebrating it with you."

I breathe in his scent, kissing him back.

His phone vibrates on the table and Dan groans.

"Let's ignore it," I whisper. He nods and lowers his mouth to mine again.

The phone buzzes insistently. I feel his hesitation and pull away. He picks up the phone and looks at the number. "It's Lizzie."

He answers the call. "Happy Christmas, Mouse!" Then he frowns and his face turns pale. "Where are you? Wait, Jenna's here too. I'm putting you on speaker so we can both hear."

There's a lot of background noise, people talking, an intercom announcement. Lizzie's voice is tight with strain, the hitch of tears in her tone.

"I'm at the hospital in Oxford in Accident and Emergency. I went to bed and left Mum drinking with Tony, but he must have gone home. I came down about an hour ago to see if she was okay and found her collapsed in the kitchen. Mum's in a coma, Dan. The doctors say her vital signs are weak and she may not last the night. You need to come now."

Chapter 11

"Of course, Lizzie." He stands up. "I'm coming right now."

"Wait, Dan, there's something else I need to tell you. The door was open to your studio so I went to check it before following the ambulance. Mum used the bar from your weight set and smashed everything in sight." Lizzie's voice breaks with emotion. "Your keyboards, the mixing deck, your computer and the microphones are all broken. She even stuck the bar through the bass drum. I'm so sorry. I didn't hear anything or maybe I could have stopped her."

Dan sinks back onto the couch, his face a mixture of anger and sorrow. "It's okay. It's not your fault. The studio is sound-proofed. She must have collapsed with the exertion."

I think of Christine's earlier rage, of how I thought

she was going to hit me. She must have channeled her anger into this violent act. I can't imagine dealing with someone like that. I put out a hand to touch Dan's arm, but he jumps up. Suddenly he is far away, caught up in his family drama.

Am I the cause of this pain? If I hadn't come to Summerfield, would Christine and Dan have argued? Would she be in the hospital? My heart thumps with anxiety. Will Dan blame me for all this?

He runs his hands through his hair. "Don't worry now, Lizzie, it's only stuff. I'm on my way right now. Hang in there."

"Jenna." Lizzie's voice is apologetic. "I'm sorry to spoil your Christmas twice over. You'll remember this one, for sure."

I bend forward to speak into the phone. "Not to worry, Liz, and I'm so sorry about your mom. Take care of you."

She hangs up, and for a moment, there's only the crackle of the fire breaking the silence between us. Dan takes a deep breath and sighs.

"I have to go, Jenna. Mum needs me. I know she seems like a strong person, but it's mostly an act. For all her faults, she's vulnerable. I have to take care of her."

I go to him and put my hand on his arm. "Of

course, you must. Dad and I have always fought a lot, but our families are the most important. I understand."

He goes upstairs and I hear him hastily packing his bag as I carry our mugs into the kitchen. I tidy the couch and check the fire is safe behind the fireguard. Just something to do until Dan comes down again and grabs his coat.

We stand by the door, his hand on the latch. "I'm sorry to miss our Christmas Day together, Jenna. But I don't think you want to spend it at the hospital."

"I don't think your mom would be too pleased to see me anyway." Dan opens his arms and I step into his embrace. He buries his face in my hair and holds me tight, like he's clinging to me, after years of this conflict. I stroke his back, feeling taut muscles under his shirt, wishing I could do more to help him.

After a moment, he pulls away. "Will you be okay here on your own?"

"Of course, I'll be fine. Go … and drive safely now."

He kisses me one last time and walks out without looking back. I close the door against the cold, then stand at the window and watch as the lights of the Jeep disappear into the darkness.

The cottage is cold without him. I shiver, feeling

the chill of winter in my bones as I secure the cottage and head upstairs. I climb into Maggie's guest bed alone and pull my cuddly little bear close. He's the only Dan I'll be waking up with tomorrow.

* * *

Gray light fills the guest room next morning. The house feels empty and I lie in bed listening to the creak of beams and the rustle of the trees outside as the winter wind blows. It's Christmas Day and I'm alone. I wanted independence, but this isn't quite what I had in mind.

I check my phone but there's no message from Dan. There are Merry Christmas texts from Dad and Maggie, Susan, and friends in Seattle and Boise. I sit up in bed and text them all back. I don't want to tell them I'm on my own, so I just send enthusiastic Christmas messages and gush about how lovely the cottage is.

There's an email from my brother, Todd. But before I can open it, I hear a soft voice calling from the back garden.

"Come on, lovelies. Come on!"

I go to the window and look out. The voice seems to be coming from Maggie's little shed. I pull on jeans and a thick sweater and go downstairs.

In the sitting room, everything looks sad, so I switch on the lights of our little Christmas tree. I put on warm socks, red gumboots, and Maggie's coat from the boot room, then go out the back door to the shed.

Selena kneels on a burlap sack next to a brown cardboard box, surrounded by canvases and tins of paint. This must be where Maggie paints, but what is Selena doing?

"Good morning."

She turns with a welcoming smile. "Morning, Jenna. Happy Christmas. Come and look, do you have these in Idaho?"

I kneel by her side and look in the box. Five tiny creatures with soft spines and long snouts snuffle next to a saucer of water, crunching tiny kitten biscuits.

"They're like mini-porcupines. What are they?"

"Hedgehogs. They're endangered and these are below six hundred grams. If they hibernate, they'll starve and won't wake in the spring. I'm feeding them up, so they might just survive."

"They're so cute." I push the dish of food closer to the smallest.

"Is Dan still asleep?"

I sigh. "No, Lizzie called early this morning. She

found Christine unconscious and she's at the hospital in a coma. Dan went there last night."

Selena pats my arm. "I'm so sorry about that. Christine has always been volatile. I don't know her well, but Maggie mentioned she's been acting strangely recently and refuses to see a doctor." She stands up. "Okay, I need to see to the vegetable garden. Do you want to help with snail throwing?"

"What's that?" I laugh and stand up.

"It's a strange English gardening ritual Maggie and I practice instead of laying down poison." Selena smiles and hands me a small tin bucket. She closes the shed door and I follow her into the garden. We walk between the raised beds of winter vegetables as she explains. "Adult hedgehogs eat the slugs, but we have to pick the snails off the plants. Maggie and I are organic gardeners, and this is actually fun!"

Selena lifts a kale leaf, picks off a snail, and drops it into her bucket. I lift the next leaf and find another one, dropping it into my bucket with a clang.

"Is Christine a close friend of Maggie's?" I ask, as we progress through the garden collecting snails.

"They roomed together in college, and since Harry and Dan are such good friends, they saw a lot of each other when the kids were younger. Maggie is Lizzie's godmother and a loyal friend, even when she doesn't see eye to eye with Christine."

Selena leads me to the end of the garden, which looks out onto fields. She takes a snail out of her bucket and points. "See that big bush? You have to throw your snails over it."

She launches a snail in a high arc and it lands neatly in the bush. With a grin, I try but it falls short. "That one will be back." Selena laughs and I have another go at it. This time the snail soars right over the bush.

"Great throw!"

We hurl our snails, one by one, until the buckets are empty. I can't help but laugh at how ridiculous we must look. "It's certainly an original way to spend Christmas morning!"

"Are you okay on your own?" Selena asks, as we walk back to the cottage. "The Potlatch is closed today, but you can join Tom and me for lunch if you're lonely?"

"Thanks so much, but I'm fine with my own company today. I've got all the food we bought yesterday, and I want to talk to my family. Besides, Dan might come back later."

Selena gives me a hug. "Well, let me know if you need anything. You know where we are."

She heads back to the Potlatch and I check the hedgehogs again. One seems to be asleep in a corner of the box, breathing softly, little eyes tight shut.

The other tiny hedgehogs squeak as they munch, and I'm comforted by them. The world is so much bigger than our individual lives, and whatever happens, life goes on. I think of Blue, his mane streaming out behind him in the wind as he runs. Animals live in the moment, and I need to do the same.

I go back inside and make coffee, then open the email from Todd.

Hi Jenn,

Sorry not to have been in touch earlier. It's been frantic since San Diego. My best friend, JT, was mugged on his way home from work just before Christmas and his hands are badly cut. He's an up-and-coming sushi chef, and his family wanted him back in Tokyo where his uncle's a micro-surgeon. I asked the hotel for some time off to accompany him to Japan, but they fired me instead. I was ready to move on anyway, so it's not such a bad thing.

So I'm in Tokyo now, staying in JT's tiny apartment. He's had surgery and is recovering in a clinic. I'll be starting work at his family restaurant in the new year.

You said that you're traveling for a bit, so how about a visit to Japan? We had no time to talk at the wedding and I'd be glad for some company right now. What do you think, little sis?

Hugs, Todd x

I sit for a moment, staring at the screen. It's too soon to go back home to Idaho. I haven't seen or done anything yet, except perhaps make a fool of myself over Dan. I don't want to stay in England if we can't be together. I'll only be thinking of him all the time. I've never considered going to Japan, but why not? After all, Dan's supposed to leave for Australia soon, and it looks like he'll be looking after his mom until then.

There's something I like about being on the move. It's as if a gate has opened in my mind. At home, we let the young steers out for the first time after the winter snow melts. They hesitate at first, staring at everything, scared of what might be out there. One musters up courage and goes through the gate, then the others follow in a rush. They love being out in the fields. It's how I feel now, that sense of new-found freedom. I don't want it to end too soon.

Before I can second-guess myself, I get online and book a ticket for Japan.

Chapter 12

My flight is later tonight. No point in hanging around, after all. I forward the itinerary to Todd and he replies quickly, saying that he'll be there to meet me. I arrange for a cab and tidy Maggie's lovely cottage. It's been a short visit, but hopefully, I'll be back another time.

In the sitting room, I look at the comfy couch and remember how special it felt to cuddle with Dan there last night. I sigh and carry our little Christmas tree into the kitchen, placing it on the cool window ledge along with a note I've written for Selena.

I put off texting Dan, because I don't know what to say. I keep typing words and deleting them. Too emotional. Too needy. Too long. In the end, I settle for simplicity.

Dan,

Thank you for the time we had together. I hope your mom gets better soon. I know you need to be with her this week, so I'm going to Tokyo to see Todd. Take care of you.

Jenna xx

* * *

Dan calls just as I complete check-in at Heathrow. My heart leaps as I answer.

"Hey." His voice is soft.

"Hey, yourself." I'm grinning like a mad woman in the middle of the airport but I don't care. He called me. He cares. "How's your mom?"

"Amazingly, she's out of the coma and even opened her eyes, which is a good sign. She's sleeping now."

"You must be so relieved."

"Yes. Her doctor said that her current medication reacted with the alcohol, putting her in a psychotic state. I'm so sorry you had to see our family like this, Jenn."

I lean against a wall listening to his voice as people stream past me. Couples hold hands and kiss goodbye, people are crying with happiness as loved ones return. Airports are emotional places and I wish Dan were with me.

"Families are complicated," I whisper. "I miss you, but you need to concentrate on looking after Christine. I remember how much my mom needed me when she was sick."

"Thanks for understanding. I miss you, too."

"Will you still go to Australia?"

He hesitates. "I don't know. It depends on how things go over the next few days. In a way, Viv's glad Mum is in the hospital. Mum refused to see a specialist before, but now we'll find out exactly what's wrong and what the options are. I'll know more in the next few days. How about you? Why is Todd in Tokyo?"

I tell him about the micro-surgery needed on JT's hands, about Todd losing his job in London and the opportunity in Tokyo with JT's family.

"I'll be thinking of you. I've always wanted to go to Japan. Send me pictures and stay in touch."

I have this soft feeling at his words, like the tearing of newly baked bread. My senses are flooded with sweetness and I want to be in his arms. How can I fly away from him?

A muffled murmur of voices comes behind him. "Sorry, I've got to go. The doctor is here. Safe journey and we'll speak again soon."

"Love to Lizzie, and I'm glad your mom's pulling through. Bye, Dan."

The line goes dead and although I'm surrounded by the bustle of the airport, I'm alone inside. I take a deep breath and walk to the gate.

* * *

It's twelve hours nonstop from London to Tokyo, but it's no hassle in the luxury of First Class. I'm super-grateful for Dad's gift. First Class is amazing, but it sure puts a big dent in my travel money. I'll need to review my finances for the next adventure, wherever that might be. Economy class on the next flight, for sure, but for now, I make the most of the luxury. I relax, watch movies, eat and sleep. I find myself weeping at a romantic movie, thoughts of Dan running through my head, memories of how it felt to be in his arms.

The plane lands at Narita International and once through Security, I immediately spot Todd, his head and shoulders high above everyone else. He waves and strides over.

"Jenna!" He folds me into a big hug. "You look fabulous. Whatever you did in London, keep doing it."

Japanese people flow quietly around us, like a river around rocks. I realize that we're in their way. Two tall Americans, used to a lot more personal space.

"Sorry, sorry." I say as Todd grabs my bags and I'm suddenly aware of how different everything is here. I don't understand any of the signs and that makes it feel far more foreign than England.

"How was England?" Todd asks.

"I found London strangely un-English." I know Todd will understand the culture clash after being in London for so long.

"What did you expect? Something out of Jane Austen?" Todd teases me as we walk.

"No, I expected it to be more –"

"Harry Potter?"

"British," I say, decisively.

Todd smiles. "I love London. It's an amazing mix of cultures and cuisines from everywhere in the world. You can be anonymous or make a name for yourself. You can be anyone." He takes my hand and squeezes it. "I didn't believe you'd come, Jenna. Yet here you are, looking like my kid sister from Idaho, but more beautiful and sophisticated. Someone gave you the best makeover ever."

I give a little twirl, letting my beautifully styled hair swing out around me. "Looking back over the last few weeks, I've changed a lot." I want to tell Todd about Dan, but perhaps there's nothing to tell?

Outside the terminal, we thread our way between Japanese people on the sidewalks. It's a dull winter morning, colored only by flashing neon signs. Todd guides me to the airport transfer bus for central Tokyo. Our luggage is stowed and we climb aboard.

"The apartment is in Nishi-Shinjuku." Todd points to the distant central city as we leave the airport. "It's a business district with the highest skyscrapers in Japan."

"I'm looking forward to seeing it." I turn to him. "But tell me more about why you're here, Todd. Why did you lose your job like that?"

He clears his throat, awkwardly. "I never told anyone at home but after Mom's death, I was close to alcoholism. You were much younger, Susan had her kids, and Dad was a wreck." He touches my arm. "I only got through the day if I was drunk every night. Bars are open 24/7 in London, so it was a way to kill the hours before I could lose myself at work again. It was controllable at first, but I was running on auto-pilot. Work, alcohol, pass out, repeat. Things began to slip and I made mistakes."

Todd stares out of the window as we travel through the outskirts of Tokyo. "JT helped me when I was at my lowest. He covered for me when I messed up at work and he took me to AA." He turns back to me, his expression earnest. "I'm sober now, Jenn. But I owe JT, and when he got hurt I wanted to help him in return."

Todd has always had an air of jolly banter and never opened up to me before. Or perhaps I was so wrapped up in my own life that I failed to notice how much my brother was hurting. I squeeze his hand gently as he continues.

"Leaving London is a good thing. It's kicked me out of a rut. JT says we're going to reboot his family restaurant and I'm starting to love life again."

"I'm so pleased, and I'm sorry if I haven't been a good sister."

Todd leans over to kiss my cheek. "Dad needed you on the ranch. I could never have helped him with that. So you've played your part, for sure." He stands up. "Here we are, time to get off."

We climb down from the shuttle to a big paved courtyard. Todd grabs my bags.

"We'll have a fabulous Japanese dinner tonight, but I can't face miso soup, rice and pickles for breakfast. We need an American breakfast and coffee."

So much is alien here but when Todd leads me into an American-style coffee shop, it's almost like being back home. We sit down in a red vinyl booth. The table opposite has four Japanese preschoolers drawing with colored pencils, supervised by two young caregivers in neat uniforms. They speak rapid Japanese to each other while scrolling quickly down their phone screens.

The three little girls have identical braids, white shirts and blue skirts, white ankle socks and black shoes. The boy wears a white shirt with blue shorts. He watches me with as much fascination as I watch him. Todd orders and then returns with familiar, packaged food and coffee on a tray.

"School's started, so it's quiet in here. Usually, it's impossible to get a seat."

The little boy looks at me then sticks one of the colored pencils up his nose. I return his look, deliberately not smiling. He's a mischievous one, no doubt of that. His care-giver extricates the orange pencil from his nostril and gives him a green one to color with.

Todd and I eat, and the boy begins to sway, one way and the other, his red metal chair more precarious with each swing. The Japanese care-giver sits him straight again and points to his coloring book. Todd leans forward to say something to me, but I miss it as the boy dives off his chair. I jump up to help but he's on his feet, shrieking and running for the door, chased by one of the caregivers.

"What was that about?" Todd's laughing, but before I can answer the remaining Japanese girl replies in perfect English.

"He says you are Darth Vader. But he is bored, so we will go to the park now." The girls pack their books into identical backpacks, then line up to bow. "Sayonara."

Todd bows and repeats the word. I bow and copy him. He waits till they've gone and then sits down again, hooting with laughter.

"Darth Vader! That's a good one, Jenn. The smooth black helmet of your hair, black coat like a cloak, black jeans and boots. I see it!"

I take a sip of coffee. "Thanks! I didn't stand out much in England, except for my height. How can I be culturally acceptable in Japan when I'm so tall and look like Darth Vader?"

"Japanese etiquette is about respect. We're okay when we show respect. You bow instead of shaking hands." Todd demonstrates. "We lower our eyes politely and speak in quiet voices. I'll teach you some easy things to say. Let's put them on your phone."

He teaches me *Konnichiwa* for hello, *Arigatou* for thank you, and possibly the most important for busy streets when I will inevitably bump into people, *Sumimasen*, excuse me or sorry.

My pronunciation is dire, but I keep practicing as we carry my bags across the paved area. Todd uses a key card to enter the tall apartment building and we squeeze into the narrow elevator. It rises swiftly to the twenty-second floor where there are

four identical doors, one on each side of the elevator shaft.

"Here we are, 224." Todd pushes open the door
and points to a small mat. "Shoes off."

I slip off my boots and realize that we're already
in the apartment. The whole place is smaller than
our kitchen back home and I feel the walls closing
in on me.

"This is … interesting."

Todd grins. "At home, we've land aplenty, but
Japan is made up of mountainous islands. Not much
land for building, so they focus on miniaturization.
This apartment has all the modern conveniences;
it's just much smaller than we're used to."

He points. "This is the kitchen. That's the refrig-
erator, this is the microwave." He gestures around.
"That's the sink and waste disposal, you stand here to
cook, and this sliding door opens to the bathroom."

"Oh, my goodness," I gasp as I peep inside. "It's a
closet!"

Todd laughs. "It's a wet room, with a shower in
the ceiling and a drain in the floor. When you take
a shower, remember to put the toilet tissue in this
plastic bag and hang it behind the door."

"Okay. What's that?" I point to a square green
box in the corner with two steps.

Todd pats it enthusiastically. "Ah, this is a Japanese

bathtub. Totally fabulous. Shower first and when you're clean, climb in and sit on the seat inside, relax and soak in the clean water. JT says Japanese people are horrified at the Western practice of getting into a tub to wash, then soaking in the dirty water."

"It does seem odd, when you put it like that." But everything seems odd to me right now.

Todd parts a bead curtain on the left. The sitting room is narrow and runs the length of the apartment with a small window on one side and another at the end. It's a relief to see some natural light.

"This is a tatami mat." Todd squats down to touch a long woven mat running down the center of the room. "It's valuable and must never be walked on with shoes. We eat at this low table, sitting on cushions. I still find it difficult to get my legs underneath, but I'm getting better."

How can I possibly get my legs under something so near to the ground? Jetlag is making everything seem fuzzy and unreal. It's completely different from England and different again from home.

I walk to the window and look out over the city. Lights flicker beneath a thin layer of mist and I can just make out tiny people streaming through the streets. How insignificant I am in this mass of humanity. What on earth am I doing here?

Chapter 13

"Amazing, isn't it?" Todd is enthusiastic. "What do you think?"

I put my arm around my big brother's waist. "I'm glad you're happy here, but I'm exhausted. Can I take a nap before we go and explore?"

"Of course." Todd opens the slatted wooden doors of a closet to reveal rolled futons and quilts. "During the day, the bedding is stored in here." He pulls out a futon, a wooden slatted bed with a thin mattress. It looks like a torture device, compared to my comfy bed at home.

Todd sees my look. "They're surprisingly comfortable. I'll wake you later to go for a walk and out for dinner."

He swishes a bead curtain half-way across the room and I lie down on the futon, pulling the quilt up to my chin. It's just long enough for me. I think about how life is so different in other countries. Even things we take for granted, like at home, we have streets on a grid system, numbered logically. In London, the streets have evolved over time, twisting and curving, with centuries-old names like Fleet Street and Pigsty Hill. In Tokyo, the streets don't even have names or numbers. I pull my little bear closer as I drift into sleep.

* * *

It feels like only minutes later that Todd wakes me with jasmine tea in a delicate porcelain cup, but I feel refreshed. It's amazing what sleep can do.

"Come on, Jenn. I'm taking you to the second-highest skyscraper in Tokyo."

I get ready quickly and we go outside. It's raining, and Todd holds a big black umbrella over us as we stroll along, arm in arm. My eyes are drawn to the colors and sounds of people in the busy streets, taking it all in. Electronic street signs in strange and beautiful Japanese lettering reflect ribbons of vibrant red and blue light through the puddles. Unusual smells drift from the food shops. People slurp ramen noodles and pick chicken off teppanyaki skewers. Then the rain starts to hammer down and we run, laughing, for the restaurant.

In the elevator to the forty-fifth floor, Todd and I are the tallest. It feels as if we take up too much room as Japanese people crowd in around us. But everyone is polite and I begin to relax as we reach the North Observation Deck. Todd and I stand close to the glass.

"It's spectacular," I whisper as we look down at the lights of Tokyo.

And it is. But I long for the open skies and pastures where I ride with Blue. I crave the forest where there are no people, not millions of them crushed together like in this massive city.

We're shown to our table and Todd scans the menu. "This is not where JT would bring us, but I think the food's excellent and reasonably priced. JT is a chef in Japanese haute cuisine, and he uses wagyu beef. You should look it up, Jenn. 'Wa' means Japanese and 'gyu' means cattle. It probably has a lot in common with Idaho organic beef. It's a luxury here. There's so little land to graze animals, so they import a lot."

"Might be a market for us. I'll look it up, and tell Barb."

We have sashimi and sushi with tempura seafood. A real feast. Todd orders a Japanese Sapporo beer for me and a soda for himself. He lifts his glass to mine and we toast our family. Then Todd leans closer and grins wickedly.

"Okay Jenna, out with it. At Dad and Maggie's wedding, you looked like my ranch hand little sister and you were miserable. You had no plans to travel. Now, you're a world traveler, all sophisticated with a great new haircut. Tell me everything."

I blush and take a sip of beer, wondering how much to tell him. "Well, Dad gave me some money, for all the time I've worked at the ranch."

"That explains the travel, but not the transformation, or the new light in your eyes. I've never seen that before."

I take a deep breath. "Okay … Did you meet Dan Martin at the wedding? The son of Maggie's friend, Christine. Tall, dark –"

"– and handsome?" Todd finishes my sentence and nudges me.

A blush rises high on my cheeks as I nod. "Well, we hit it off. He was leaving for England that morning so I took a chance and went with him." I look out over the city, then back to my brother. "I've never met anyone like him before."

Todd shakes his head and grins. "Ah, those British men. Really, Jenn, I understand. I had an English girlfriend for a while. So, what happened? Are you two an item now?"

I shake my head. "No. His mom had an accident and ended up in hospital, so that cut short our time in England. And Dan is leaving soon to work in Australia, so there's no hope for us."

I stop talking as our food arrives. Fragrant miso soup and crispy tempura with vinegar and chili dipping sauce. Delicious! And it's so good to talk with my brother again.

"I can't stop thinking about Dan. I haven't had a crush on anyone since high school."

Todd laughs. "Oh yeah, Calvin Wilson, I remember. Every girl in Boise had a crush on him. But this sounds more serious. Are you falling in love?"

I take another sip of my beer, my mind reeling with confusion."Yes, maybe. I don't know. What about you? Have you ever been in love?"

Todd's face softens, and he smiles ruefully over the rim of the lacquer soup bowl. "Just once. There was a girl called Gloria at boarding school, before I went to Paris for the Cordon Bleu course. We were close until we graduated." He shrugs his shoulders. "But her parents split us up; rightly, I suppose. We were too young and just starting out. Gloria went to college in New York, and we were desperate being apart, for a while. We wrote and called for ages. But then Gloria stopped talking to me and I found out she had married a guy in Philadelphia. I've met other girls, of course, but the job of a chef is always full-on. It's a lot of hours, and relationships don't last. I've never loved anyone like I loved Gloria, but the distance finished any chance we might have had together."

I nod. "That's probably what will happen to Dan and me. Two people on different journeys going in opposite directions."

I take a tempura prawn and crunch it, forgetting my sorrows with delicious food and Todd's company. Then my phone pings with a message.

Todd leans over to look at the screen. "Ooh, it's from Dan. You have to read it."

I open the message.

Hi Jenna, I hope you're doing well. I have mixed news. Mum's been diagnosed with early-onset Alzheimer's disease, but with care and medication, it can be managed. Aunt Viv is going to help Lizzie, and they want me to go to Australia as planned. I miss you and hope you're having fun in Tokyo. Dxx

I show Todd. "That's it then. He's going and it's all over."

"Not necessarily. He could fly this way to get to Australia. Why not ask him to change his ticket and have a stopover here? We could go to Kyoto or something. It's soooo romantic." Todd's laughing but my heart leaps at his suggestion.

"Do you think Dan would go for it?"

"Nothing to lose. Ask him."

I shake my head. "He's short of money. He won't be able to afford it."

Todd puts his hand on mine. "Jenna, quit making excuses. If Dan wants to come, he'll find a way. Let's walk home." He settles the check with the waiter. "*Gochisōsama deshita*. Thank you for the feast."

We take a last look at the amazing views and retrace our steps to the apartment. This time, I no longer notice the lights or the people. I just want to see Dan's face and be in his arms one more time.

As soon as we're back in the apartment, I text him with the idea.

I lie down on the futon, hugging my bear, unable to sleep until I hear back. The minutes stretch on.

Then finally, a text!

Dear Jenn, Thanks for the invite. It means a lot. I've managed to change my ticket. Arriving Narita Airport 5 a.m. local time the day after tomorrow. Okay to meet me? xxx

Oh my, I'm so excited that I roll off the futon and rattle the bead curtain to wake Todd. He gives me a sleepy smile.

"Sure looks like love to me, Jenn. Now, get some rest."

* * *

The morning his flight arrives, Todd and I leave the apartment at 4 a.m. on the Tokyo Metro to get to the airport on time. I've seen videos where guards in white gloves cram people into tightly packed trains, but it's not that bad. It's a culture that pretends not to look, but I still feel like the early morning freak show. I'm relieved when we get to the coffee shop next to Arrivals. I get the breakfast wraps while Todd looks at train schedules for Kyoto.

"We need to book seats online for the *shikansen*, the bullet train."

"I'll get them, Todd. You're not working right now and it's a chunk of change for three of us."

We buy the tickets and then wait, watching the Arrivals screen. Dan's flight is processing and I think of him in the line for Passport and Security. Is he as excited as I am?

Todd taps quietly on his laptop, looking at buses and temple timetables for Kyoto. I scan each group as the doors open. Then I see Dan. I can't help the smile that blossoms on my face and I run to him.

Dan sees me, his eyes bright with joy. He drops

120

his bag to catch me and hold me in his arms, stroking my hair as I cling to him.

"I missed you, Jenna."

"I'm so glad you're here." I pull away and suddenly I'm embarrassed. I didn't even realize how much he meant to me until this moment. Now I don't want to let him go. He bends his head to kiss me, and I lose myself in him.

Todd walks over. "Guys, you're embarrassing me and about a million Japanese people!"

"Sorry." We break apart, breathless. Todd shakes hands with Dan and we make small talk about the flight as the three of us cross the concourse. I don't want to let go of Dan's hand. Every time I look at him, a smile blossoms on my face. Is this what being in love feels like?

We take a cab to Tokyo station and Todd stops the driver at the apartment to drop off Dan's bigger bags.

As soon as the cab door closes behind him, Dan gently pulls me into his arms and kisses me. The cab driver unfolds his newspaper and disappears behind it.

I touch Dan's dear face with my fingertips. "I can't believe you're here."

"I'm so glad I came. I thought maybe what we felt would quickly fade, but I've missed you so much. I don't want to leave you again, Jenna, but my flight to Australia is tomorrow. We have only twenty-four hours to be together."

Chapter 14

His words stab through my heart, so I lean in to kiss him again. "We'd better make the most of them."

The door opens, Todd gets back in and we head to the train station. When we arrive, I bow to the driver and give him a super-large tip.

"*Sumimasen, arigatou gozaimas.*"

The driver's grin and Todd's astonishment make me laugh. We walk onto the platform to find the bullet train waiting, a long, sleek beauty in blue and silver.

"Awesome!" Dan's clearly impressed as we climb aboard and find our seats. "This is more like an aircraft than a train."

"It travels at two hundred miles per hour." Todd looks at his watch. "We'll be in Kyoto in two hours and twenty minutes."

We hang our coats on little hooks by our seats and at the exact time of departure, the train whispers out of the station. I'm by the window, next to Dan, my hand firmly in his. Todd sits opposite us. The train passes through early morning suburbs and rice fields. Then the world becomes a gray-green blur outside as the train accelerates to top speed.

"It's interesting that the train tracks here are left-facing." Dan is reading the train information leaflet.

Todd leans back in his seat, hands behind his head. "People drive on the left here too. When Japan needed a railway system in the nineteenth century, France, America and Britain bid for the contract. Britain won, but if it had been France or America, the railways and roads in Japan would be right-facing."

"History is bizarre." I close my eyes, resting my head on Dan's shoulder, enjoying his arm around me, rocked by the lullaby of the train. I'm warm and I close my eyes to rest, half-listening as Todd and Dan chat.

"So, why are you going to Australia, Dan?"

"I've got a teaching contract in Queensland, but it's more about seeing my dad. He and my mum split up when I was young. I went to visit him in Sydney when I was fifteen, but it's thousands of miles away and ten years have rolled by. We email and phone for birthdays, Christmas, and times like that, but nothing beats seeing each other in person. Charlie, my Dad, lives in Cairns with his second family."

"Sounds like you have a good relationship, even if you can't see him much," Todd says quietly. "My dad and I never saw eye to eye, especially when I was a teenager. I wasn't what he wanted as a son. He wanted someone like him, a rancher and a business-man. But I loved to cook with Mom and Grandma." His voice softens. "I'm so glad that Jenna took on that role at the ranch. Dad needed her."

Dan's arm tightens momentarily. "She's definitely special." The train hums along the tracks. "I guess I was lucky, then. I only had a few years with Dad, but he was my best buddy. When he left, I was so unhappy, but I spent a lot of time with Harry, Maggie's son, and that helped. You met him at the wedding. But Jenna said you lived in Oxford for a time, before she was born. You must have done some exciting things with Greg then?"

"Some," Todd agrees. "Dad had a big job with North Sea oil. He was based at headquarters near Oxford, but he was in Scotland a lot and traveled to other places. We saw him about as much as we did in Boise. Susan was ten and happy at her school. I was seven, and my school was heavily into sports. I hated sports and my accent made me an outsider, so I didn't do so well. Dad saw that as another of my failures. But Mom was lonely in England too … Then Jenna saved us."

My eyes flick open. "I did? How? I wasn't even born."

Todd throws back his head and laughs. "We had a great holiday in Italy, then Mom found out she was pregnant, so we all went back to Boise. My new baby sister took the pressure off me."

"Funny, it was the opposite for Lizzie and me," Dan says quietly, knowing I'll understand. I gently squeeze his hand, and he squeezes back.

"Susan and I took Jenna everywhere, to keep her out of trouble," Todd continues. "She used to toddle along between us holding hands or we'd sit her up on one of the old horses. We gave in to her on most things, or she'd start crying. And boy, could little Jenna howl if she didn't like something!"

I sit up and glare at him. "It wasn't all perfect for me, you know. When I went to elementary school, you weren't around to protect me. The other kids said I should be on a reservation. Sue was at Stanford, you went to school in Philadelphia, and I got left behind and bullied."

Todd frowns. "Sorry, Jenn. But I had to get away. I begged Mom to let me go. Maybe you don't remember, but Dad and I fought all the time."

I remember.

"I was into fashion and music," Todd explains to Dan. "I colored my hair, got tattoos, put studs in my nose and ears. Mom sighed and said it would be okay in the end, but Dad exploded every time he saw me."

"You and Greg seemed to be okay at the wedding?"

Todd nods. "Time heals a lot, I suppose, and we've both moved on." He pauses. "Now Dad has Maggie, and we don't need to worry anymore."

A train attendant wheels a lunch cart along the aisle. Todd buys water and boxes of sushi for lunch. After we've eaten, I'm sleepy and pillow my head on Dan's shoulder.

"Sorry, it's the train," I murmur faintly. He holds me and I drift away as the train races toward Kyoto.

I wake when we slide to a halt. The carriage is full of excited chatter from the tourists and Japanese people alike.

"Hey, Jenn." Todd grabs his bag. "You still snore like you used to at home."

I'm mortified and jump up, combing my fingers through my ruffled hair. "Why didn't you wake me?"

Dan holds my coat, so I can slide my arms into the sleeves. "He's teasing. You were snuggled up like a little dormouse, totally silent."

I make a face at my infuriating brother. Todd grins, leading us off the train and into a bus station nearby. He's done his research and knows where we're going. We'd be lost without him because all the signs are in Japanese.

Todd pays the bus fare and Dan and I look out at the streets of Kyoto. It's all urban streets at first, and we can't see any temples. Then we get off the bus and Todd leads us between high walls. We step around a corner into another world.

A pagoda gate stands shaded by Japanese conifers. Its layered tiers are painted red and white, a portal between the ancient and modern city. Then the sun breaks through the clouds and rays of light filter through the trees. It's beautiful and I'm so glad to be here with Dan.

It's winter-cold but cheerful as Todd leads us along winding gravel paths. "Kyoto is the spiritual center of Zen Buddhism and has over two thousand temples. This one is smaller but a great example of Japanese aesthetics. Many temples have dry landscape gardens called *karesansui*. They're mainly white gravel, raked in patterns to give the impression of water to focus the mind and help you meditate."

We stroll along a boardwalk beside a garden of raked stones, then Dan and I sit down under a cherry tree holding hands. Todd wanders off, leaving us alone. The Zen gravel waves are raked in symmetrical lines and I gaze at them, seeing patterns in the movement. Rings of ancient trees, the neat lines of our cattle pastures, and Blue standing at the fence with his herd of mares. Even so far from home, nature takes me back to the ranch.

Dan squeezes my hand and I wonder what he is thinking. Does he miss his home? There's so much to say, or perhaps there's no need to say anything at all. Every second together is precious. I should be appreciating the cultural beauty of the temples, but I just want to sit here with Dan. We cuddle up on the bench, bodies pressed as close as can be in a public temple garden.

Soon enough, Todd's back. "How about a walk through the bamboo forest?"

We take another short bus ride and enter the Arishiyama Bamboo Grove. Giant bamboo stems meet high above us like a roof of feathery fronds. Soft, green light filters through and it's like walking on an emerald planet. Todd walks on ahead, and there's no one else around in our little grove. Dan stops and takes me in his arms, his hazel eyes green in this light. He brushes the hair from my face.

"Jenna," he whispers and bends to kiss me. Nothing else matters and when he lifts his head again, we are both breathless. "It's heaven to see you, but it's going to make leaving again even more painful."

I hug him tighter as thoughts of following him to Australia cross my mind. But I stay silent. I couldn't bear it if he said no. And even if I went, what would I do there? We would only have to say goodbye yet again.

We follow Todd, our heads tilted back for the last sight of the bamboo forest as we emerge on the other side. We go to a small tea house and drink green tea from pretty cups. It's refreshing, but I'm definitely up for some good coffee soon.

Todd's phone buzzes and his face lights up. "It's JT." He scans the message. "The surgery was successful and his next check-up is in four days. He's going crazy and wants to come back to the apartment and go to his appointments from there. Sorry, sis, it looks as if I'll have to find you a hostel. But don't worry, that will be fun. Loads of younger tourists hang out there and you'll find some new friends."

"Hmm, okay, sounds good." I nod but my mind is whirling. I don't want to stay in Tokyo if I'm not with Todd. I'm too scared to travel around Japan on my own with no understanding of the language. I can't meet Dan's eyes right now. I want to be with him, but I can't force myself into his new life.

We finish our tea and catch the bus back to the bullet train. This short time together has been sweet torture, and as the minutes tick by, I find myself without a direction. What shall I do now? Where shall I go?

Chapter 15

"Thirty minutes until we're back in Tokyo." Todd's words hang over me like an ominous cloud. I clutch Dan's hand even tighter. His warmth comforts me, and his sweater smells faintly of incense from the temples. He puts his arm around me and pulls me close, whispering into my hair.

"Why don't you come with me?"

I sit up, leaning back from him. His eyes are bright, the question in them sincere. "Really?"

"What?" Todd asks.

Dan takes a deep breath. "I was thinking that maybe Jenna could come with me to Australia. I emailed Dad and Angelina from the café. They've replied and say they'd love to meet her." He pauses and looks at me. "That's if you want to, Jenn? There's loads more to see in Japan, and I don't want to interrupt your travels. But I have a week before I start teaching, so maybe we could do some exploring in Cairns together?"

A huge smile spreads across my face. "Of course, I'd love to go with you. That would be amazing."

I hug Dan in delight then we get on his phone and start looking for flight options. It will definitely be Economy for me this time, as I need to make the money last longer. When the bullet train arrives at Tokyo station, we get a taxi back to the apartment to collect our bags.

"Thanks for arranging the trip, Todd." Dan shakes my brother's hand. "It was brilliant."

"Me, too." I call as I fold clothes carefully back into my black Dorchester bag. Who would have thought I'd get so meticulous about packing?

I take the remaining yen from my wallet. I was expecting to stay longer and spend the money with Todd as I know he must have limited savings and has lost his London job. Now, I slip the money into an envelope and write on the outside.

Dearest Todd,

Please accept this with my love, toward a new start in Japan. I've had an amazing time and am so happy to have found my big brother again!

Thanks for everything and I'll talk to you later.
Jenna xxx

I tuck it into the futon, so that Todd will find it when he cleans up later.

At the airport, Dan and I pick up my tickets and check in. Todd hugs us both and stands waving farewell. "Safe journey and let me know how things go in Australia!"

Dan leans in to kiss me as we wait in line for Security checks. "I'm glad we're together again." As we kiss, I cross my fingers, hoping that nothing bad happens this time, like it did on Christmas.

After passing through Security, we have time to kill before the flight, so we wander around the airport stores.

"Let's find some toys for my little brothers and sister." Dan tries out every car that transforms into a dinosaur. They are pretty cool and we have fun choosing two of them. We find a little Japanese doll in a geisha outfit for Ellie, his little sister. All the gifts are done as our gate number is announced. But Dan guides me toward one last shop.

"Before we get on the plane, we need to get you a few essentials, since you have yet to experience the joys of long-haul Economy travel."

I'm intrigued as we walk around the store with a shopping basket. Dan puts in a pair of long black flight socks. "To prevent deep-vein thrombosis."

My eyes widen. "That wasn't an issue in First Class."

Dan laughs. "That's because you can put your feet up or lie down." He adds an inflatable neck pillow, throat drops, earplugs, and an eye mask.

"Wow, thanks." I'm a little worried. How bad can this flight be?

We head to the gate and finally board the plane, turning right into the Economy seating. Dan is near the front of the section but my late ticket purchase means I'm sitting two rows from the back, near the restrooms. The flight is full and people push and shove around me, fitting their carry-on bags into overhead compartments. I find my seat and stare in horror. It's a tiny space between two other people, like a sandwich filling between two slices of bread. There's no way I can fit in there, not with how tall I am. My legs are way too long.

But there's no choice.

The guy on the aisle stands up to let me in and I fold myself into the seat, trying to get comfortable as the plane prepares for take-off. Nostalgically, I compare flying First Class and close my eyes, imagining myself there now: Welcomed on board by cabin crew with chilled champagne; large comfortable seats with ample leg room; the choice to lie down and sleep whenever; wonderful food from an extensive menu any time you want it; and large restrooms with expensive toiletries. Bliss …

Dad used to say that if you can afford to fly First Class, he couldn't see why you would ever choose anything else. But of course, most people can't afford to do that. Dan's on a teacher's salary that would never stretch to it.

The Economy in-flight meal is served and then the cabin lights dim to encourage people to sleep. I turn from side to side, knees pushed up against the seat in front of me. Then it reclines another two inches and cramp twists my right calf into a rope of agony. I yelp with pain, throw off my blanket and try to massage it straight again. The guy on the aisle looks sideways at me as I pant and knead the muscle.

"Sorry, I have to get up." I say through gritted teeth. I grab my backpack and water bottle and he stands to let me slide out.

I bite my lip to stop myself from screaming as I try to stretch my leg, but the pain is so intense that I can't even put it on the floor. I hop down the aisle through the gloom, the only illumination from the small screens on the back of seats. There is a space by the emergency door at the rear of the plane. I stand there stomping the affected leg and then kneel on my left knee, frantically massaging my right calf muscle.

"Are you okay?" A flight attendant looks down at me. Her voice is concerned, but her eyes betray detachment. She's seen this before.

"Do you have any painkillers?"

"I'm sorry, we are not allowed to give out medication." She reaches behind and grabs a miniature chocolate bar. "Maybe this will help?"

I laugh at how ridiculous this is, but then I think of Dan leaving me in Tokyo or going back to Boise without him. Staying in Cairns with him will make all this worthwhile. I just need to hang on and survive – for another nine hours. I'm scared about going back to my seat, so I read and walk laps around the Economy section, up one aisle and down the other.

Time passes slowly. I walk by people waiting in line by the restrooms, next to the only place I can stand out of the way. Vacant. Engaged. Vacant. Engaged. A constant stream of faces, some of which I begin to recognize as the minutes and hours tick by.

Now and then I go to look at Dan, hoping he'll be awake so he can come and talk to me. He's in a center-middle seat, worse than mine, with two people to climb over to get out. But his eyes are closed. He's retreated into himself, listening to his music or just asleep.

I return to visit him every hour, on the hour, but Dan never moves. With his blanket tucked up to his chin, and legs stretched out under the seat in front, he appears comatose. I've been standing for hours, with excruciating pain in my leg and no sleep. If looks could kill …

It feels like forever, but eventually the announcement comes for landing. I squeeze back into my seat, acutely aware that we have another flight from Brisbane to Cairns. I am not looking forward to that.

I hobble off the plane and meet up with Dan in the Transfer Lounge. "You look rough, Jenn. Bad night?"

I feel pathetic telling him about my leg, but he gives me a gentle hug. "Poor you. But it's just a short hop to Cairns. Hopefully you won't have to get back on a plane again for a while after that."

On the little plane for the final leg, I try to disguise my fatigue with make-up. I'm a little apprehensive and want to look good when I meet Dan's family. After all, my meeting with his mom didn't go so well.

"It's going to be fine." Dan takes my hand and reassures me. "They'll love you."

We walk through to Arrivals and the doors swing open. Dan looks around and then waves at a family, who all wave back enthusiastically, big smiles on their faces. We head toward them.

The tall, older man must be Dan's dad, Charlie. He has the look of a boxer past his prime, with all the rough edges smoothed out. Next to him is a petite Chinese woman, his wife, Angelina. Two dark-haired boys jump up and down with unbounded energy, and between them is a little girl in a wheelchair.

Chapter 16

"Welcome to Australia, Dan." Charlie hugs his first-born child. "It's been far too long."

Both men have tears in their eyes, and I feel privileged to witness this special moment in Dan's life. Then, there are introductions all around.

"This is Angelina, Matt, our eldest, and Adam."

"And this is Eloise." Angelina bends to gently wipe the little girl's mouth with a cloth bib tied around her neck.

"We call her Ellie," Matt chimes in. "Look at my Batman toy, Dan. Pow!"

Dan ruffles his little brother's hair. "That's awesome." He puts his arm around me. "This is Jenna, my friend from America."

"America," Adam says. "Where they make cartoons?"

His eyes are wide, and I can't help but giggle. Ellie makes a sound, arms waving around as if trying to get our attention.

I squat down in front of the wheelchair and smile into her dear little face. Dan told me that Ellie is six years old, but he didn't tell me that she had special needs. She is so tiny, she looks younger than age six. I hold her hand gently, and her eyes dart all around. Her spiky black hair stands up in all directions and her other arm waves randomly.

"Hello, Ellie."

She makes a sound, and I see interest in her eyes. Angelina squats down next to us. "She likes you. That's Ellie's way of saying that she wants you to stay here and talk to her." She looks at her daughter. "We'll talk to Jenna when we get home, sweetie."

We head out to the parking lot with the luggage cart. Charlie does wheelies with Ellie strapped into her wheelchair. She's grinning and shrieking with joy as the two boys zoom around her, pretending to be airplanes. I smile at the mayhem. This feels much more like a normal family life than the conflict of Home Farm back in Summerfield.

We all climb into Charlie's family van, which is equipped for a wheelchair and big enough for the kids and us. We drive out of the multi-story parking garage into bright afternoon sunshine. Back home, the trees are bare in the northern winter, but here, tropical flowers bloom in vibrant colors – purple bougainvillea, creamy jacaranda, and carob trees with huge seed pods hanging down. I'm excited to explore this new place with Dan and squeeze his hand as we drive.

Twenty minutes later, we turn into a subdivision. It's similar to the US, with big houses standing on their own lots and three-car garages. I'm relieved that everything won't be in miniature like Japan.

Charlie parks and immediately, Matt and Adam open the car doors and are off, shooting at each other. "Pow! Pow!"

Angelina calls after them. "Boys! Change into your togs, please. Don't get those Sunday clothes dirty."

The boys zoom upstairs, shouting and tumbling about as Dan and I carry our luggage into the hall-way. Then they run past again, this time in swim-ming suits, which I now understand are their togs. I'll have to get used to Australian slang.

"They waited so patiently at the airport," Charlie says, as he follows the boys. "Now they need to let off steam in the pool. Come and join us when you're settled in."

Angelina pauses on the wide staircase, Ellie on one hip. "Your room is up here, Jenna."

I follow her, carrying my bag through a hinged baby gate at the top of the stairs. A young Chinese woman is waiting and she gives me a shy smile. "Hi, I'm Pearl."

Ellie reaches out to her and Angelina passes her over. "Pearl is Ellie's care-giver, she's part of our family." She raises her eyebrows at the noise from the boys shouting from the pool "As you can hear, Jenna, we need all the help we can get!"

Ellie is making impatient squeaking noises. She leans out of Pearl's arms toward a wicker basket of toys. I reach down and pick out a bright pink My Little Pony with a platinum mane and tail.

"Is this what you want?" I hand it to her. Ellie hugs it and makes happy noises.

Angelina looks at me in surprise. "How did you know that's her favorite?"

"Because it would be my favorite too. I'm a horse fanatic."

She shows me to the lovely guest room with its own bathroom, beautifully decorated in shades of sea-green. Through the window, I can see a gleam of bright blue ocean.

"I'll leave you to freshen up."

There's the sound of enthusiastic splashing from the pool and I lean out of the window to see Dan and Charlie in with the boys. It's the first time I've seen Dan's muscular torso. His skin is milk-white next to Charlie's tan, but I can't take my eyes off him. He's laughing and so happy to be with his dad and little brothers. It's as if father and son have never been apart. I think of Todd and our dad, how they never shared moments like this. But all families have their different dramas, that's for sure.

I'm looking forward to playing with the children, but maybe not today. I'm feeling shivery, probably over-tired from the flights, so I'll skip the pool for now. I think of Ellie and send a quick message home on my phone.

Hi Barb,

Dan and I have arrived safely in Cairns! His family are very welcoming. I'll write a long email tomorrow, but just wanted to ask if you could look in the old toy box under my bed? Dan's little sister, Ellie, LOVES My Little Pony toys, just as I did. Could you send the ponies plus the stable and horse trailer? They'd make Ellie really happy. Love to you and Uncle Doug.

Jenna xxx

I unpack and have a shower, pull on jeans with a clean t-shirt, and go back downstairs with the gifts we bought for the children. The sun is setting behind the palm trees and Charlie is lighting the barbecue. An aromatic smell of garlic and ginger marinade wafts from the kitchen. Dan is out of the pool now, a multi-colored sarong tied around his waist. The long skirt would be considered strange for men back home, but it seems normal in the tropics. He pulls on a t-shirt and comes over with a couple of beers. His eyes are shining as he hands me one.

"It's so good to swim after that long flight." He clinks his beer against mine. Then he shakes his wet hair at me and I shriek with mock horror. He puts his arms around me and I sink into a moment of bliss.

"Dan and Jenna up a tree," Matt and Adam chant, spotting us. "K-i-s-s-i-n-g."

They fall about laughing, and we give them the gifts to distract them. "They're from both of us," Dan says.

Within minutes, Matt and Adam transform the vehicles into dinosaurs. They rush over to demonstrate them to Charlie as Pearl comes out of the house carrying Ellie. She's sweetly bathed and ready for bed, wearing a pajama set with shorts and a sleeveless top with My Little Pony transfers on the front. Angelina helps her unwrap our gift, but the Japanese doll seems inappropriate now. I wish we'd bought her something else. I hope Barb will send the package soon.

"It might be a bit old for her," I explain, but Angelina smiles.

"It will look lovely standing on Ellie's shelf with her books. Thank you."

Charlie takes his little daughter from Pearl's arms. "How's my princess?"

He gives her a soft kiss on the cheek, and she snuggles into his arms. Then he carries her around the table for a goodnight kiss from each of us. I touch the pony logo with a gentle finger.

"Goodnight Ellie. Sleep tight."

Charlie takes her upstairs while Dan tends the barbecue. I love to see him here, surrounded by his family. In the kitchen, Angelina's chopping knobby, pale-green fruits for dessert. I pick one up.

"What are these? I've never seen them before."

"Custard apples, deliciously sweet and just coming into the markets in Cairns. Tell me what you think."

She hands me a piece. It's an explosion of flavor and as I swallow, the sweet juice soothes my throat. It's been feeling raw since the plane journey, but the custard apple helps.

"Wow! That's good. I look forward to more after the barbecue."

I sit down to help her. "Dan told me that you're a nurse? Is that in the hospital here?"

Angelina nods. "I used to be in hospital nursing, but now I work part time at the eye clinic. It's flexible hours which helps with Ellie, and I love being out doing something professional again, after having our family."

"That sounds amazing." I pause. "I guess I'm thinking about what I want to do next. I've been helping my dad at our ranch and could take that on as a career, but I've also got some other ideas." I look out at Dan, now chatting happily with Charlie. "Dan's sense of purpose with teaching makes me want to do something that helps people."

Angelina smiles and touches my arm. "We all have to find our own way, Jenna."

Dan and Charlie are grilling fish and I hear Charlie ask, "How's Lizzie doing, Dan? She knows I tried to get your mum to let her visit, doesn't she?"

"Yes," Dan hesitates. "But things are ... difficult. Lizzie is helping to look after Mum now that she's sick."

Angelina bends closer to me, her voice quiet. "You've met Dan's mother?"

I nod, still slicing fruit.

"You like Christine?"

I don't know what to say. I'm acutely aware of the

politics of Dan's family, but I like Angelina and I feel welcome here.

"Let's just say, we didn't see eye to eye." I grimace.

Angelina giggles. "I've heard so many of the stories. Jenna, I think we'll be friends. Please call me Angie."

We grin at each other and I set the table. The boys are sent to wash their hands, then Charlie and Dan bring platters of barbecued seafood to the table. Angelina asks a blessing on our meal and everyone digs in.

"This is barramundi." Charlie points to a thick fish steak, which smells amazing. I take a small piece plus a giant prawn and some salad. But my body aches and my stomach rebels at the thought of food. I need to lie down or I might fall over.

"Are you okay, Jenna?" Dan frowns. "You're looking pale."

"I didn't sleep on the flight so it must be jet-lag. I'm sorry, do you guys mind if I go up to bed?"

"No worries." Angelina walks with Dan and me to the door. "Sleep well, and we'll see you tomorrow."

At the door of my room, Dan rocks me in his arms. "I'm sleeping on the pull-out bed in the study, Jenn. Come down if you need anything. Dad's arranging for a small apartment near the school for me, but I'm staying here for now."

"Sorry to break up the dinner party."

"Not a problem. Dad and Angie are super relaxed. It's the Australian way. You sleep now." He kisses my forehead. "I'm so glad you're here."

I drift off to sleep with the sound of Dan's happy voice below my window, laughing and joking with his family. I wish I could be down there with them, instead of up here feeling like death warmed over.

* * *

I wake in the middle of the night, sneezing violently, with what feels like razor blades in my throat. My joints ache, and my head is pounding. I must have picked up a virus on the flight, and it's kicking in with a vengeance.

I go to the bathroom and sink to the floor, holding a damp towel against my head, to try and ease the pain. Tears fill my eyes. I just want to go home.

Chapter 17

There's a quiet knock on the door.

"Jenna, are you okay?"

Angie's soft voice is concerned and I open the door to see her standing there, wrapped in a cotton robe.

"I'm sorry to wake you," I whisper, wiping my eyes. "I must have caught something on the plane."

"Don't worry, I'm often up with Ellie in the night. I'll get you some painkillers and hot tea for your throat."

I stumble back to bed, grateful for her help.

A few minutes later, Dan comes up, wearing pajamas. He carries a steaming mug of tea, a glass of juice and a large box of tissues. "You must be feeling rotten. I'm so sorry, Jenna. Angie says to take two of these tablets every four hours."

"I'm sorry you had to be disturbed as well," I croak as I gratefully sip the tea.

Dan sits on the bed and strokes my back in gentle circles. It eases my cough and I lean into him. This is not how I pictured our romantic, tropical getaway. I must look terrible but right now, I feel so bad I don't care.

"It's okay, I wake easily and go back to sleep just as quickly." He brings me another cool washcloth from the bathroom. "I used to help at a night shelter in London. I'd be up and down all night."

I lie back and Dan places the washcloth gently over my eyes.

"Thank you," I whisper. "The painkillers are kicking in and I think I can sleep again. How come you didn't get sick traveling in Economy?"

Dan squeezes my hand. "I've only ever flown Economy, Jenn. I'm probably immune to bugs. I'm going back to bed now, but text me if you need me and I'll come back up."

He closes the door softly, and I drift into sleep, comforted by his caring.

∗ ∗ ∗

The next morning, I wake when the sun is already up. Golden light fills the room. My body still aches and I sneeze explosively, grabbing tissues to blow my nose.

There's a knock at the door and Dan pushes it open with his foot. He looks great, wearing tan slacks and a white shirt, a man at ease in the tropics. He sets a tray down next to me with fruit juice and tea, toast, preserves and a vacuum flask filled with more tea.

"I thought you might want to eat something. You definitely need to drink lots today."

Matt and Adam appear at the door carrying scarlet hibiscus flowers. "These are for you, Jenna." Adam lays them across the bottom of the bed. "We picked them from the garden to say get well soon. Mum's taking us to the last week of Holiday Sports Club now."

Matt grabs his brother under one arm, scrubs his head with his knuckles, and runs off downstairs. Adam runs after him, yelling. I can't help but laugh and it triggers a gigantic sneeze. I'm not a pretty sight.

"Thanks, Dan, and please thank Angelina for me."

He bends to kiss me, but I ward him off with one hand. "Stay away, I don't want to infect you."

He steps back. "Okay then, but you concentrate on getting better. Dad and I are going to look at an apartment today, and then I'm going to the school to meet the Principal. Angelina and the kids are out all day, so you'll have quiet. Sleep, and I'll be back later. You need to get well. I want to go exploring with you."

He goes out and I listen to the bustle of car doors slamming and engines starting as everyone leaves. Finally, the house is silent. Birdsong filters in from the yard and sunlight dapples the ceiling. I take more painkillers and settle down to sleep again.

* * *

When Dan gets back from town later that afternoon, he brings me a fruit smoothie. "Lots of local mangoes in there."

"Yum, I'm starting to feel a lot better. How was your day?" I sit up in bed while Dan sips his coffee.

"The Principal was great. It's so laid back here compared to England. I'm teaching a Year 6 class, plus math and music. They've got loads of instruments." His eyes sparkle with enthusiasm. "There are three teachers who form a band now and then, so I'll be able to play. Maybe even get back into writing my own music."

I think of his studio in Summerfield and the instruments Christine smashed in her rage. It's good to know he can start again here. "I'm so glad you've found a job you love, Dan."

"My granddad used to say that we need something to work for, something to hope for, and someone to love."

His words echo around my head as he comes over to show me some pictures on his phone.

He said *love*. Could he mean me? I bite my lip, hoping he'll say more, but he scrolls down to show me more images of his day.

"This is the small apartment Dad's rented for me. It's behind the golf course and looks toward the ocean. I can't wait for you to see it. Oh, and there's a staff trip the day after tomorrow before school starts. We're going snorkeling on the Great Barrier Reef." He pauses dramatically, then grins. "You're invited too. But only if you're well, of course."

I look up at him and smile. "I wouldn't miss it for the world and I feel a lot better. I'm hungry, too, which is a good sign. How about I shower and come down for dinner?"

I'm determined to be okay for the trip out to the Great Barrier Reef. After all, I'm in Australia with this gorgeous man. Enough of the sick bed, it's time for adventure!

Charlie leads the applause when I finally make it

downstairs, and Ellie bangs her plastic sippy cup on her high chair.

"We're so glad you're better." Charlie pulls out a chair for me to sit down.

"Thanks so much for looking after me."

Charlie puts his arm around Angie's shoulders and they look at each other with such love. I smile to see their obvious affection. Might Dan and I ever share a look of love like that? Charlie looks down at his petite wife.

"When I first met Angie, I was sick in the hospital in Sydney and she was one of my nurses. It was love at first sight ... or maybe just a high temperature?"

"Oh, you!" Angelina pushes him away. "Matt, tell Jenna where we're going tomorrow to celebrate her being well again."

Matt puffs up his chest. "It's our best Saturday trip. We go to the top of the mountain on the SkyRail, right through the tops of the trees. There are white cockatoos and enormous butterflies."

He spreads his hands, thumbs crossed in the middle to show the size of the butterflies. Adam echoes his gesture and bursts out, "Sometimes we see big lizards, and we come down the mountain on the little railway. It's awesome!"

Angelina puts out cold cuts and salads on the dining room table. We hold hands and Charlie asks a blessing. I feel at home and finally well enough to join in Dan's family life.

* * *

The next morning, I wake up thinking of the rainforest and look out of my window, excited about our day. I can hear the kids downstairs and Dan's deep laughter as I dress. It's good to hear him so happy after his previous family conflict. Summerfield seems so far away now.

After breakfast, we step outside the air-conditioned house into the heat of the Queensland summer. It feels like I'm breathing thick syrup instead of air and sweat immediately pools at the base of my spine.

Charlie sees the look on my face. "Guess you don't have it so hot and humid in Idaho, Jenna. It's tropical living at its finest here!"

I dive into the air-conditioned car and breathe in the cool as we drive to Kuranda, northwest of Cairns. Charlie points at the dark green forest ahead.

"These are the oldest continually surviving rainforests in the world. They once covered the entire Australian continent."

We arrive at the SkyRail station and board an

open-sided gondola, like a ski cable car but with a clear glass floor. It bumps a little at the beginning and I reach for Dan's hand as my stomach does a flip. Then we lift off and travel right through the rainforest canopy.

The smell is intoxicating, a heady mix of exotic flowers and the earthy scent of abundant forest. Huge yellow butterflies feed on purple fruits and tropical birds dart among the trees, calling with whoops and whistles.

I gaze down into the many shades of green, finding it strangely comforting that these trees have been here for thousands of years and will continue, regardless of the drama in my own small world. I look at Dan and smile. We need to make the most of the time we have together. He smiles back and leans over to kiss my cheek. "Happy?"

"Very happy."

In the Aboriginal village at the top of the hill, we wander around booths selling crafts, fruits and herbs from the forest. It's my turn to push Ellie's wheelchair as we go into the butterfly house. We all laugh with delight as we're covered in multi-colored butterflies. It's magical. I can feel their tiny feet on my skin.

After lunch, we take the scenic railway back down the mountain, with spectacular views of forest and waterfalls all the way. It's been an incredible day, and by the end of it, my nose has stopped running completely. I'm all set for the Barrier Reef tomorrow.

That evening I help Angie prepare dinner. From the kitchen window I see the gardener outside, Pearl's husband, wearing thick gloves. He bends to pick up a horrible bulbous creature from the lawn and puts it into a bucket.

"What on earth is that?"

Angie looks out and makes a wry face. "Cane toad, brought to Queensland from Hawaii in 1930, to control beetles on the sugar crops. But they've bred, taken over, and are highly toxic. People round here kill them in various ways, but I'm a Buddhist, as are Pearl and Lee, so he relocates them for us."

She taps on the window and waves. Lee waves back with a smile and continues to pick up toads. "Australia is a paradise in so many ways, Jenna. But there is a dark side, too – fire, flood, dangerous animals, venomous snakes and spiders, and tropical diseases. It's not all sunshine and flowers, but that's how it is in life."

I turn her words over in my mind. Loving Dan is joyful and yet risky, especially with his difficult family situation back in England. But then I think of Mom and Dad, and the many happy years they had together before she died. The pain and loss our family suffered at her passing doesn't diminish our happy memories. Must I accept the danger of loving Dan in order to find happiness?

Chapter 18

It's just after dawn the next day when Dan and I arrive at the marina for our trip to the Great Barrier Reef. I'm introduced to his school principal, Stephanie, then to a colleague, Josh, and his wife, Brittany. There are a whole group of friendly people, whose names I promptly forget, but there are two female teachers whose greetings are distinctly frosty.

Megan and Ashley are both as tall as me, with long blonde hair and lithe golden bodies, clad in bikinis and cut-off denim shorts. They're the only single women and are clearly attracted to Dan. I suddenly wish I'd brought something other than my plain black swimsuit.

"Welcome aboard the Coral Sea Star." A tanned and smiling Australian hunk invites us to sit on lockers around the deck and passes out bottles of water.

"I'm Brandon, and this is my brother, Austin. We own and operate this commercial reef catamaran out of Cairns to the Great Barrier Reef. It's a true wonder of the natural world. 2,300 kilometers long with 3,000 individual reefs and 900 islands."

Austin takes over. "We're going to have an amazing day, guys. Snorkeling on different parts of the Reef, then a break for lunch on Green Island. It's jellyfish season, so we have some stinger suits for you to wear. But no worries, we'll have fun!"

The sky is cobalt blue and the ocean sparkles a thousand shades of turquoise. It's already hot as the catamaran motors out of Cairns marina, but there's shade when Austin and Brandon raise the sails. They flap, pull taut, and we gather speed. It's exhilarating!

Dan and I sit together in the bow, listening to the swish of water and the song of the wind in the rigging. I marvel that we're here together, looking out over the Coral Sea in Australia.

We soon reach the first snorkel site and there's excited chatter as everyone puts on stinger suits, masks and fins. I'm feeling a little nervous and remember Angie's words about the dangerous side of Australia. "What about sharks?"

Brandon overhears my question. "Only small reef sharks here, nothing to be worried about." He helps me into a stinger suit that covers everything to my wrists and ankles. "This will stop any tiny jellies, so you can just enjoy yourself."

Dan helps me with my mask. "Just remember to breathe through your mouth."

I'm a strong swimmer but more used to rivers than the ocean. I've never snorkeled and my heart beats faster as I stand on the back deck. Then we're in and once I put my head under, it's pure magic, like being in an enormous tropical fish tank. The warm water cushions me, and I begin to breathe more easily.

Dan swims beside me, pointing out parrotfish and a giant clam with fleshy blue lips around an iridescent shell. Orange and white clownfish weave in and out of the anemones. Then I'm astonished as an enormous purple fish with pouting lips and bulging eyes swims right by us! Dan grins at me through his mask and takes my hand as we swim to the drop-off at the reef edge. Something primal pulls at me from the dark blue deep. It's the same as galloping along the ridge with Blue, a sense of being on the edge of nature.

When we finally climb back onto the catamaran, I'm beaming from ear to ear. "That was fantastic!"

Everyone talks excitedly about what they saw and

I learn that the monster purple fish was a Maori wrasse. Then we motor to Green Island.

Dan and I sit to eat our lunch in the shade of palm trees, looking out at the ocean. Megan and Ashley walk over to join us, spreading their towels and lying down.

"Is this too hot for your English skin, Dan?" Megan says as she rubs sunscreen into her bronzed skin. "The sun's fierce here: we have one of the highest rates of skin cancer in the world, so we teach Slip, Slop, Slap to all the kids. Slip on a shirt, slop on sunscreen and slap on a hat." She holds the bottle up to him. "Shall I put some on your back? You don't have a natural tan like Jenna."

She looks over at Dan and he blushes a little. "No, I'm fine, thanks. I'll just keep my shirt on." He turns to me. "The sun's not a problem in England or Idaho, is it, Jenn."

Ashley pipes up, blue reflective sunglasses hiding her eyes. "Isn't Idaho where they grow potatoes?"

I want to groan out loud but rein in my annoyance at the stereotype. "Yes, but my family has a ranch north of Boise where we raise beef cattle, surrounded by mountains and wilderness. The sun's not a problem, but we have lots of snow in winter, gun accidents, bears, wolves and occasionally, white-water wipe-outs when we're rafting."

"I've always wanted to go rafting," Dan says as he finishes his lunch.

Ashley smiles flirtatiously at him. "We have rafting here in Queensland, Dan, and it's warm. I can take you. There are Grade 3 rapids on the Barron River or Grade 4 on the Tully ..."

A hot wave of jealousy sweeps over me and I interrupt her. "We have Grade 4 and 5 white water."

Then I stop myself. What am I doing, trying to compete with her? I lie back on the sand, trying to relax. I breathe deeply and gaze up through the palm fronds. "But Idaho has gentle experiences too, like floating the Boise River in big tire inner tubes."

The crew are collecting the lunch boxes. Dan gets up and brushes the sand from his shorts. "Fancy a short walk, Jenna, before it's time to sail again?"

I smile and take Dan's hand as we walk away from the Aussie teachers. Holding hands, we wade together in shallow turquoise water along the white sand beach. Gentle waves roll in and the water is cool on my legs. I bend to pick up a small piece of coral and it's like tiny white flowers petrified into stone. It fits into the palm of my hand and I'd love to keep it as a souvenir of today, but I replace it in the same spot and look up at Dan.

"Take only photographs."

"And leave only footprints." Dan smiles as he

finishes the slogan for me and we walk to rejoin the group.

Once under sail for the trip home to Cairns, Dan and I lie in the net between the hulls of the catamaran. The boat leaps through the green water like a flying fish, spray sparkling all around us. I laugh with sheer joy as dolphins suddenly appear on both sides of the boat, riding our bow wave. It's been the most perfect day with Dan. I don't want it to end but when it does, I know I'll treasure these happy memories.

* * *

That evening after dinner, Dan and I sit with the family on the upper deck in the cool. Ellie sits on my knee, looking at a picture book of animals. I point and say the words, then she tries to copy the sounds.

Angie carries a big parcel out from the house. "This came for you today, Jenna."

"Oh good! It's for Ellie. The Japanese doll wasn't something she can play with, so I asked my Aunt Barb to send some things from home. I hope that's okay?"

"Of course." Angie and I open the package with Ellie and she squeaks with excitement as the little ponies tumble out. I smile as she reaches for my old favorite, a blue pony with a rainbow mane and tail. I quickly assemble the stable and play with her on the floor. We trot the ponies in and out of the stable until she's so tired, her eyes are closing.

"Thanks, Jenna," Angie whispers as she picks Ellie up to carry her to bed. "That was the perfect gift."

I put the toys back into the box and Dan comes over and puts his arms around me. "Thank you for doing that, Jenn. You're so sweet with Ellie and I love watching you play with her." His eyes are soft. "You're great with kids. Maybe you should think about teacher training?"

It's not something I want to do, but Dan's words bring home our situation. He'll be working full time from now on and I'll only see him when school finishes for the day. He also has sports and band practices, preparation, and marking to do. I can't stay here with his family for much longer, and I need something to do. I need to apply for a work visa, but should I stay here if I don't know where this relationship is going?

And what about the ranch ... and Blue?

I turn to kiss Dan and my doubt melts away in his arms. For now, I'll make the most of the time, so I'll help Ellie with the thing I know most about.

After dinner, the family sits on the deck to relax

as the cicadas croak from the yard. I sink into a chair with my phone.

"What are you doing?" Dan glances over my shoulder as I search the web.

"Looking for a riding teacher for Ellie. There are stables that help kids with special needs, and I'd love to take her. Would that be okay, Angie?"

"That sounds amazing, and she'd love it. Matt and Adam are so active and we do lots of outdoor things with them. Can we go and look for a stable tomorrow, while Dan is teaching?"

* * *

The next day, Charlie drives Angie, Ellie and me out to a farm that advertises riding for special needs children. It's not far from Cairns and has a small teaching ring under shady trees. The yard is well-kept and the owner, Nicki, is kind and competent.

"Our ponies are well-fed and well-trained. There's no biting or bad behavior with the children."

Angie looks relieved at this and Ellie goes crazy when she sees the ponies. It's worth everything to see her little face so happy. Nicki gets out a special harness, then Charlie lifts his daughter onto a small chestnut pony.

"This is Socks." Nicki leads the pony and with

Charlie supporting, they walk slowly around the ring.

Angie has tears in her eyes. "Look at her face, Jenna, she's in heaven. Thank you so much for suggesting this. I don't know anything about horses, so it's something we never would have tried without you."

I give her a hug and she wipes away her tears. We take lots of photos. Ellie loves every minute and I'm so happy to see her smile. But being here reminds me of what I miss about home.

Once we're back, I download the photos of Ellie, study them and begin making a sketch of a saddle. I've never done anything like this before, but I can picture what she needs to make riding a better experience for her. The saddle needs to be like a child's high chair with removable panels at the back and sides. It must support her, but also stimulate muscle development. Ellie loved being at the stables today, but she won't be able to take riding any further without special equipment. I finish the sketches, take photos and email them to Barb. Maybe she knows a saddlemaker who could build it for me?

That night, I tell Dan about my idea as we sit out later by the pool in our swimsuits.

"That sounds amazing." He kisses me on the

forehead. "You have hidden depths, Jenna. You keep surprising me."

It's hot and sticky, so we slip into the pool again. Palm trees rustle in the faint breeze as we stand shoulder deep in the water. Dan takes me in his arms and together, we gaze up at an inky sky, dotted with enormous bright stars.

"The stars in the Southern Hemisphere are so different from home."

Dan points. "That's the Southern Cross … and there's the constellation, Carina. You can see so much more from here, even without a telescope." Dan looks at me and we kiss. Passion sparks between us, but there's also sadness. The call of a night bird echoes across the yard as Dan lifts his head.

"Oh, Jenna. What are we doing?"

I lean into him. "Enjoying the night air together in paradise."

But I know what he means.

I have no place here. School is in full swing and Dan will be gone more often. The pull of home gets stronger as Cairns gets hotter, and I long for the cool rain and snow of Idaho. There's a tug on my heart, toward Blue and the ranch. As much as I want to be with Dan, I need to go home.

Chapter 19

"I want you to stay," Dan whispers. "But I need to make a go of this contract. Jenna, I never planned for … this. For you."

His words warm me and our bodies curl around each other in the cool water. "I know. But I can't stay and just be waiting when you get home every day. I need more than that. I'm struggling with the heat. I miss my forest. I even miss the rain."

Dan laughs. "Yeah, I never thought I'd long for a drizzling English day."

I roll away from him and float on my back. "I miss riding out with Blue under the wide Idaho sky, the wind whipping my hair. I miss working on the ranch and being physically tired at the end of a hard day. I'm going crazy in air-conditioning all the time."

Now that we're talking about it, I realize how much I've been holding back.

"I miss Barb and Doug. Dad and Maggie will be back from their trip now and spring is when the foals are born. I want to be there … but I don't want to leave you."

I stand as tears well up in my eyes. Dan brushes them away with gentle fingers. "There are days when I'm homesick too, Jenn, but I'm busy all the time. There's no future for me in England, and Aunt Viv says it's better for both of us if I'm away from Mum. I'm committed to this contract and the kids here need me." Only the rhythmic sounds of cicadas punctuate the silence between us before he continues.

"But no one has ever tugged at my heartstrings like you do. On the deck at Maggie and Greg's wedding, you looked up at me through that tumbling curtain of hair with those huge sad eyes and said …"

I giggle. "Who are you and why are you talking to me? Then I vomited."

Dan takes both my hands in his, laughing. "But then somehow you changed into beautiful Jenna Warren, serious and soulful one minute, charming and sparkling the next. I want to be with you, but the timing is just all wrong."

I lift my arms and put them around his neck, pulling him as close as I can. I rest my head on his chest and he traces patterns on my back, sending shivers down my spine. We seem to be splitting up, but we were never even really together.

"I'll get my ticket tomorrow," I whisper. My words are heavy. I'm desperate to go home, yet I long to stay.

Dan sighs and then smiles. "How about we take one last trip together? Make some more beautiful memories before you go?"

I look up into his clear hazel eyes. "I'd love that."

* * *

When school finishes on Friday, Dan comes to get me and we drive north along the Captain Cook Highway to Port Douglas. Our hotel perches on the edge of a lagoon overlooking the ocean, and at dinner we toast our adventures in England, Japan and these last few weeks in Queensland.

At dusk, we walk along the beach holding hands, talking, laughing, determined to seize the day.

"I've booked your dream ride for tomorrow, Jenn. I'll call you just before dawn."

He kisses me goodnight and I fall asleep to the sound of the ocean.

Early the next morning, we drive to the trekking stable. Will, our guide, fits us with safety helmets and we meet our horses.

"You're both experienced riders and the only ones going out this morning, so we'll have a great time. This is Blaze, your horse, Jenna. Dan, this is Mr. Ed. He's a big guy and sometimes pulls when he's excited, but he's better for your weight and English riding style. Just watch him when we get on the beach. He likes to take off!"

Dan and I mount and then Will brings out a stunning palomino mare with a cream mane and tail. With only a light halter – no saddle or bridle – he leaps onto her back and I grin with delight. "That's how I ride Blue, my Appaloosa."

Will turns in a tight circle using only knee pressure. "Really? I've been training Apricot for the past three years. She works pretty much with my voice now."

We talk about horses as we ride out of the shady yard across fields into the Daintree Forest. We fall silent along the forest track and I just enjoy being here with Dan. I ride with loose reins and murmur quietly to Blaze, who flicks her ears back and forth.

Suddenly, we emerge from the sun-dappled trees onto a pristine, white sand beach. In the far distance, the rainforest stretches toward Mossman

Gorge and the brilliant ocean sparkles to the horizon. Crystal waves whisper along the shoreline.

Will walks Apricot onto the sand. "We have it all to ourselves. So, a Brit, a Yank and an Aussie rode onto this beach at Cape Tribulation –"

"Sounds like the beginning of a joke." Dan grins as he checks Mr. Ed. I love seeing how well he handles the horse and wish we could ride together again.

"No joke, guys," I urge Blaze on. "It's always been my dream to ride along a beach like this."

"Come on, then." Will leads us along sand washed smooth by the ocean.

Blaze delicately lifts her hooves, splashing as we walk in the shallows. Shoals of tiny fish dart away. We ride in the mirage of an ocean that mirrors the sky, and I record it in my heart, a snapshot of Dan in this tropical paradise.

"Ready to go a bit faster?"

Dan and I grin our agreement and Will encourages Apricot into a smooth loping canter. I urge Blaze to follow. Then there's an explosion of water and we're soaked as Mr. Ed plunges past. Dan is laughing on his back. "Sorry, he's full of beans!"

"Head him out into the water," Will calls, laughing as well. His pale chinos blend with Apricot's wet back and he looks like a centaur, half-man, half-horse. "The beach here is safe, Dan. You can slow him up that way."

Dan guides Mr. Ed deeper into the waves and sure enough, after a few minutes, he can hold the big horse to our pace.

"Sorry we can't swim them today." Will pulls up at the end of the beach. "Salt ruins those saddles if they're immersed. So, we'll turn up the trail here, get water for them at the Lodge, then head inland back to the stables."

"You could swim with Apricot," Dan suggests. "Seems a shame not to take her in, when you've no tack to spoil. We'll just wait here and cool off."

"You sure?" Will looks at me. "You're paying for this. I'm supposed to be making sure you guys have fun."

I smile at him. "Part of the fun would be to watch you swim with Apricot."

"Okay, thanks!" He turns the eager mare and heads back into the water. When she's in deep enough, Will slides off and swims next to her.

Dan and I sit quietly, resting in the shade with Blaze and Mr. Ed. Suddenly, there's a rustle a little way up the track. The foliage parts and a huge bird steps out. It's the size of an ostrich with eyes that look almost human and a huge, blue-horned crest on the top of its head.

"Cassowary." Dan breathes softly. "Rare, endangered and about the most prehistoric bird on the planet."

I'm astonished. From Charlie's bird book, I remember that cassowaries are solitary and territorial. They have three toes on each foot and a long nail capable of inflicting horrific injury. I hold my breath. Our horses are wary, ears forward. Behind us, Will is on Apricot's back once again and emerging from the water.

Dan and I make alarmed eye contact but remain motionless as three striped cassowary chicks step onto the track after their mother.

"That was fabulous!" Will calls, walking Apricot back to us along the beach.

The cassowary's head swivels and its big, beady eyes focus on us. There's a moment when time stands still, then she crosses the track with long, swift strides, the chicks scuttling after her.

The foliage rustles just as Will reaches us. "Was that a cassowary?"

I nod. "Utterly amazing."

"Certainly was. Good thing you guys didn't panic and move. They can take out a horse's guts with one kick. People sometimes see cassowaries at the Lodge, but it's a first for me to see one with chicks."

We ride back through the forest and water the

horses at the Lodge. We drink iced tea with staff who are amazed to hear of our encounter. Back at the stables, we say goodbye, then Dan and I set off on the drive back to Cairns.

After days of heat and perfect blue skies, the thunderhead clouds of a tropical storm are moving in over the ocean.

"Look at that huge funnel." Dan points east. "I'll try to get us home before it gets too close or we'll need to stop and shelter somewhere."

He accelerates along the empty highway under a bruised purple sky. Every kilometer is taking me closer to leaving him. Am I doing the right thing in leaving? Might there be a chance for us if I stay?

The rising wind whips palm trees back and forth. Bright flashes of lightning fork over black water and rising waves. We drive in silence, each focused on the road ahead and our own thoughts.

Then, with a sigh of relief, Dan pulls into Charlie's street, just as thunder rolls directly above us. There's an explosion of hail that pounds on the metal roof of the car. It's deafening, then cuts off abruptly as Dan drives into the garage. He presses the remote control and the electronic door rolls down, cutting off the screaming of the storm. We narrowly escaped being devoured by an enraged monster.

"Well done, you guys." Charlie appears at the

door to the house. "Angie and I were beginning to worry. We're upstairs, eating popcorn with the kids and watching the storm. Come in and get warm."

We unload our bags and join the family upstairs. The temperature has dropped dramatically and they're all curled up on couches, covered in warm throws.

"Cool storm!" The boys greet us and Ellie holds up her arms for a hug. Dan and I settle in next to Angie to watch the lightning show, as violent rain lashes diagonally across the yard.

That night, I dream of riding with Dan on a perfect white sand beach, but then black clouds speed in from the ocean and I lose him in the storm.

I sit bolt upright, breathing hard as the wind shrieks outside and rain continues to hammer on the roof.

It's too early to get up, but I can't sleep again for fear of another nightmare. I shower, complete my packing, and take my bags downstairs.

When it's time to leave for the airport, I can barely hold back my tears. Charlie and the boys stand by the door. Angie has Ellie in her arms.

"Thank you so much for a great time." I hug them one by one. "I'm sorry to go."

"We loved having you stay," Charlie kisses my cheek. "You're always welcome."

"Keep in touch, Jenna." Angie supports Ellie as she winds her little arms around my neck, making her sad noise. She's holding my old rainbow pony and I bend to kiss her cheek, and him as well.

"Keep riding, little one."

Dan carries my bags into the car and the whole family waves as he reverses down the drive. Even in such a short time, they have touched my heart and I feel the ache of parting.

In the airport Departures area, Dan and I drink coffee and hold hands, waiting until the last minute before I have to go through Security.

"I'll miss you so much, Jenna."

I brush a tear away, trying to be upbeat. "Maybe you'll come to the States sometime?"

He smiles. "Maybe."

Last call for my flight. We stand and cling to each other, our final kiss full of sadness. Neither of us expected to feel this way, but our lives are going in different directions and there's nothing more to say.

I turn away, hurry through Security and go straight to the gate. The plane is a small aircraft, waiting on the tarmac and bound for Brisbane, where I'll transfer long-haul to Los Angeles, from there, back to Boise. I walk the marked path between airline staff in orange jackets and climb the steps.

Dan said he'd be watching from the roof terrace so

at the top, by the door into the plane, I turn and raise my arm in farewell. Tears well in my eyes. I don't want to leave you, my love, but I must go home.

Chapter 20

The plane lands in Los Angeles and taxis along the runway. From my reclining seat in Business Class, I turn on my phone as the plane approaches the terminal. After the misery of flying long-haul Economy, I couldn't face it again on top of the pain of leaving Dan. The flight has at least been bearable, but I can't stop thinking about him.

My phone connects and pings with a new message. When I see Dan's name, my heart leaps. I eagerly click it open.

Dear Jenna,

It's been amazing to spend this time with you. But we've both made choices about our lives that mean we can't be together. It's better to have a clean break, so we can both move on.

Long-distance relationships rarely work, and we both need to be free.

I want you to be happy, so please forget about me and Australia. Enjoy spring at the ranch.

Always your friend, Dan

His words are like a stake through my heart, even though I'm the one who left. Tears sting my eyes but I can't sit here and weep. The other passengers bustle around me, eager to get off after the long flight, and my sister, Susan, is waiting for me. I don't want to burden her with my relationship woes as she has enough problems of her own. I bury my feelings, get off the plane and head to Arrivals.

Just before the doors, I take a deep breath and plaster a smile on my face, then step through.

"Jenna!"

Susan waves from the barrier. She's lost weight, and as we hug, I can feel her ribs through the sweater. I hug her more tightly, wanting to tell my sister how much she means to me, but we've never been the gushy type of family. I remember Todd opening up in Japan and I'm determined to be a better sister to Susan.

"You look gorgeous." She steps back to hold me at arm's length. "Is this the effect of a certain Dan Martin?"

His name makes me want to cry, so I deflect her question. "Are the girls not with you? How are they? How are things with Steve?"

Susan's face darkens and we go to have lunch at one of the airport restaurants. She tells me about how hard things have been with Steve, and recounts the ups and downs of the end of her marriage. It's been a difficult time for her and I reach for her hand.

"I'm sorry I haven't been around more."

Susan squeezes my hand. "I'm so pleased you've been traveling and having fun, Jenn. I don't want you to worry about me. I'm doing okay. I have new possibilities ahead, even though they've sprung from a lot of pain."

"How are the girls coping?"

"Steve sees them every other weekend. Shelby's finding it difficult and Skylar turns inward. She goes quiet when things are stressful, but Shelby tells it loud and clear. She's throwing tantrums about everything. It's because she's afraid, but it's wearing me out. I love my kids, but sometimes …" She screws up her face in a grimace. "Maybe you can come and stay with us soon? The girls wanted to be here today but their school doesn't like them to be absent during the week. I wanted to see you on my own for a while, so I didn't make a fuss."

I nod. "Of course, we'll work something out after

I've seen Blue and settled back in at the ranch. But why don't you guys come to Boise instead? I know you want to keep it all under control here, but grandparents, animals and fresh air might help put things in perspective?"

Susan laughs. "Listen to my little sister, quite the philosopher now! I guess you needed England, Japan and Australia to put things in perspective for you?"

We talk non-stop and I tell her all about my travels, but brush off her deeper questions about Dan. To be honest, I don't know what's happening. The time flies and soon I need to leave for my domestic flight.

Susan stands to give me a hug goodbye. "I'm so glad that you're back home, Jenn. I'll call Dad and arrange that trip to Boise. You've been very evasive about Dan, but I want to hear more when we come to visit."

She leaves and I go to the gate. While waiting in the boarding area, I can't help thinking back to when Susan and Steve were in love. They were going in the same direction and so happy. I remember their wedding and the joyful birth of their two daughters. I saw them laughing together so many times, their eyes shining with love for each other and their family.

And now, it's all gone.

I think about Mom dying of cancer three years ago and how it devastated Dad. He left after the funeral, retreating deep into the Payette Forest to mourn her. Uncle Doug thought he might kill himself. I was furious at Dad for leaving me and angry at Mom for dying. I didn't know how to grieve, so I pushed all my emotions into a box and locked it tight. When Dad came back, a distance had grown between us. I realize now that he was just trying to survive and hold it all together day by day.

Is it worth loving someone so much when it seems inevitable that your heart will be broken somehow, someday?

I read Dan's email again on the plane to Boise. I know he's being logical to say it's the end, but my heart rebels at the thought of never seeing him again. I gaze out of the window at the blue sky, thinking of him on the other side of the world. Is he looking out at the sky in Australia thinking of me?

As the plane lands, I pull myself together. Dad is meeting me and I'm so looking forward to seeing him. Life has changed for both of us in the past few months. I push Dan's email to the back of my mind.

Through the Arrival doors, I spot Dad holding a big purple balloon with *Welcome Home* in gold letters. It's so unlike him to buy something frivolous.

I laugh and run into his arms. He's suntanned, looking fit and well. Marriage and a long vacation clearly suit him.

"Oh, Dad, it's so great to see you! Thanks for coming to meet me. Where's Maggie?"

"She stayed home so I could be here to welcome you back. She's making dinner at our apartment."

We carry my bags to the truck and I ask a million questions about their vacation, then about Blue and the ranch. We drive through the center of Boise onto the road west toward the ranch, then turn into River Point. It's a new complex where Dad and Maggie now have an apartment.

"I still go to the ranch every few days, but Doug and I promoted Hector to ranch manager. I'm taking a step back from running the business."

I never thought I'd hear Dad say something like that but he and Maggie are making new memories together. Perhaps over time, a broken heart can be mended. We drive through beautiful landscaped lawns with a view over the small lake, the sun touching the water with a golden light as it sets over the hills.

"It's a great place, Dad. I know you both wanted somewhere in town. I like the lake and all the water birds."

Dad parks and leads me up the little steps to the

apartment. I feel awkward for a moment when I walk in, but Maggie doesn't hesitate. She holds out her arms and hugs me.

"Welcome home, Jenna."

Her cheeks are flushed from cooking and her eyes bright with happiness. Dad wraps his arms around both of us. "It's so great to have you both here together."

We laugh and then break apart. Maggie walks back into the open kitchen. "All your pictures have been great, Jenna, and we're excited to hear about your travels. Come in, dinner's almost ready."

I follow her and hop up onto a stool at the counter. "Thanks so much for your gift of the keys, Maggie. I loved your beautiful cottage in Summerfield. I'm only sorry I couldn't stay longer."

My thoughts stray back to Dan and me wrapped in each other's arms by the fire. The memory seems far away now.

Dad takes a bottle of champagne from the fridge and opens it with a twist and a faint pop of the cork. He pours three goblets and hands one each to Maggie and me. We raise them in a toast.

"To adventure and Jenna's safe return home."

It's good to see them so relaxed. Many of Dad's personal things are here, brought down from the ranch. There are framed photos from the wedding on a shelf. Dad and Maggie, looking into each other's eyes, then one with Todd and me, Susan and the girls, another with Maggie's kids, Sam and Harry. Next to that is a photo with all the guests looking up and smiling at the photographer. I remember that he leaned out of an upstairs window to get us all in. I search the faces and spot Lizzie turned toward Harry with a hopeful look. Then I see Dan, his head thrown back with laughter and I touch the photo with a fingertip.

"That was a special day," Dad looks at the photographs over my shoulder. I lean back to give him a kiss on the cheek.

"I'm so glad you're happy, Dad."

Maggie brings dishes over to the table. "I heard from Lizzie yesterday. She says Christine is back home from the hospital. She goes to an adult day care center every weekday where they do activities with Alzheimer's patients." She looks at me with concern as we sit down. "Lizzie said that you had a bit of a difficult time when you were there?"

I shake my head. "It was nothing, really. I know now that Christine was sick."

Dad serves aromatic rice and Maggie passes the tasty chicken dish to me. "Apparently, Christine thinks Dan is just away at college. She keeps emails from him in her purse." She raises an eyebrow and smiles. "Lizzie also said you and Dan spent some time together …"

I blush a little and look down at my plate. "This looks amazing, Maggie. I'm starving. Tell me about your trip?"

Dinner is delicious and it's wonderful to see Dad and Maggie laugh together as they recount stories from their trip to New Zealand. I talk about my travels but manage to avoid saying much about Dan. I'm starting to feel really tired, and as much as I like being with Dad and Maggie, I need to go home. I yawn and stretch. "Sorry, guys. I'm super tired from the flight and want to see Mom and Blue early in the morning."

"Of course." Dad takes his keys from a hook near the door. "Do you want me to drive you up to the ranch? Or you can take my truck if you like?"

"I'll take the truck. Thanks, Dad." I kiss them both and they walk me to the door with more hugs.

I kiss them. "Thanks for the wonderful dinner, Maggie. See you tomorrow, good night."

I feel a growing sense of excitement as I drive the familiar road to our ranch. I took my home for granted, but going away has given me a new sense of belonging. I felt like an outsider in England, in Japan, and even in Australia where the culture is quite similar to the US. Now I know that this place is where I should be.

I pull up outside the ranch house and the dogs bound out of the barn, wagging their tails in delight to see me. I kneel down and rub them and they lick my face. I laugh and they run around me. It's so good to be back. I feed them and then take my bags upstairs.

My room is the same but I feel like a different person from the Jenna who went to Dad and Maggie's wedding in California. Traveling has given me a sense of perspective, an idea of how big the world is out there. Now I'm back, I value my home and what I have right here.

* * *

Next morning, I open my eyes to see the soft early sunlight shining across my bed. I'm in my own bed, in my own bedroom, back in Idaho. I stand at the window and gaze out, taking in the familiar view I love. I unpack the beautiful clothes from London and think of Isabelle at the Dorchester. I'm not sure I'll ever wear these lovely things again, but I hang them in the closet anyway. I put on my comfortable ranch clothes, jeans and a cotton shirt, tie my hair quickly into one braid down my back and go outside.

On the Upper Road, I sit next to Mom's grave overlooking the valley and tell her about the trip. The wind blows cool and refreshing on my face, bringing the scent of the forest. It feels so good after the sticky heat of Cairns, but I remember the warmth of Dan's arms and his kiss as we stood in the pool that night. Tears well up in my eyes again.

"I love him, Mom," I whisper, kneeling down by her headstone. "But it's over and I don't know how to move on." I can't hold back anymore and weep bitter tears for all that I've lost. But after a while, I'm calm. I feel Mom's love and know that she would tell me to take Blue and ride. She'd say God has a plan for me and that time will show me the way.

I take a deep breath and walk away from the grave along the top of the hill. The herd is a little way off and Blue stands proudly at the head of the trail, guarding them. I whistle and his head turns sharply. He answers and comes at a gallop, the mares following. They're a beautiful sight, with all their manes and tails streaming behind them.

Blue reaches me and bends his head to blow through his nostrils at me and nuzzle my hair.

"I've missed you, beautiful boy." Tears come again as I put my forehead against his muzzle and stroke his shoulder. I grab a handful of his mane in one hand and vault onto his back. Blue is part of me and he senses my restlessness. We canter along the crest of the hill and I look out over my valley. However much I'm hurting over Dan, I'm finally home.

Chapter 21

The days pass and I throw myself back into work at the ranch, helping Hector and the ranch hands. Hector had already been with us for twelve years by the time Blue was born and we know each other well. We work hard and I like coming home to the ranch house exhausted from the day. I eat quickly and fall into a deep sleep. There's no time to think of Dan much as I fill my hours with ranch work.

Winter recedes and spring comes. The Boise foothills are soon alive with wildflowers – yellow arrowleaf, blue flax and delicate purple lupin. Our cows calve and the mares have foals. Soon, I can ride without my padded down jacket and the sun is warmer on my skin. I love this time of the year, the turning of seasons from the darkness of winter into the light of spring.

Dad and Maggie sometimes come to the ranch for dinner, but I often go over to Barb and Doug's and talk ranch business. I'm learning a lot and it's invigorating. I still miss Dan and cuddle my little bear at night, but the acute pain has become a dull ache. I think of Ellie when I ride. I no longer take my freedom for granted, knowing she is trapped in a wheelchair. I'm still working on her saddle with a saddlemaker that Barb recommended. He and I email back and forth about options, but I want it to be perfect before he makes the final custom item for Ellie and I send it to Cairns.

One afternoon, Barb and I are sitting on the ranch deck, cleaning tack.

"We've got a booth at the agricultural fair this weekend, Jenn. Do you want to come with me? Maybe start learning more about the marketing and selling side of the business?"

Her words startle me. That side of the business has always been done by her or Dad, but I realize this is exactly what I want to do. The ranches are not just stock and horses. If this is my future, then I need to know about the sales and financials too. It's the next step in the journey and it feels good to want to know more.

"Yes, please. I'd love to work at the fair with you."

Barb smiles. "Doug takes a big display freezer

down, full of cuts of beef packaged in the various sizes we distribute. We chat to people, giving out promotional leaflets and samples. We get a lot of new contacts and often see results in sales."

It's a whirlwind of activity over the next few days. I learn about pricing, cash flow and marketing as we get everything ready. It's fascinating, and I can see so much potential for the ranch. I remember what Dan said about finding his purpose with teaching. Now I'm finding mine.

Early on the Saturday morning of the fair, Barb, Doug and I drive down to the fairgrounds. We set up, putting out leaflets and boards with pictures of the ranch. As I pin up quality certificates about our beef, I glance up at the hill behind. The last time I was here, I stood up there with Blue, looking down at a parade. How things have changed since then.

Barb and I are dressed for meeting clients. I'm wearing a fitted Italian white shirt and my designer black jeans from the Dorchester collection with the black Italian boots. My hair has been trimmed again and it swings, smooth and shiny, around my shoulders. I've done my makeup the way Isabelle showed me and I feel confident and excited to represent our brand to the public.

The doors open and people stream in. Soon I'm busy answering questions and taking orders. It's much more fun than I expected and I realize why Dad loves doing business so much.

Time passes quickly and at lunchtime, Barb gives me a quick hug.

"You're doing so well, Jenn. I'm going to take a break and check out the competition. You okay on your own?"

I grin. "Absolutely. See you later."

A local hotelier comes over and we're soon engrossed in conversation. But I feel other eyes upon me. I turn my head and notice a tall, blond man a few feet away. He has the physique of an American football player, strong square shoulders and a chiseled jaw. He smiles and takes off his sunglasses.

My heart skips a beat as I recognize him. Calvin Wilson! The darling of Boise High and my high school crush. I quickly turn away and continue the business conversation. But when the hotelier has shaken hands and left, Calvin strolls over. His piercing blue eyes stare into mine and he smiles flirtatiously.

"Are you interested in our organic Idaho beef?" I ask.

His eyes flick to my name badge. "Jenna." A look of surprise comes to his face. "Jenna Warren? Weren't you at Boise High?"

I pretend surprise. "Well, yes, but I don't believe we've met?"

He's slightly taken aback, as if everyone knows who he is.

"Cal Wilson." He offers his hand and I shake it but keep up the pretense of not recognizing him. He frowns and takes a leaflet. We have never done business with his family, who raise non-organic beef in feedlots. "I didn't know you were with the Daley outfit."

"Our ranch is next to the D-Bar and we're part of their organic beef operation. I've just returned from an extended trip to Europe and Asia-Pacific."

It's an enormous exaggeration, but it sure sounds good. A couple of people are now looking at the images of the ranch, picking up leaflets. "Please excuse me, Cal, I need to work. It was good to meet you."

He puts a hand on my arm, his smile dazzling. "Can I call you? Maybe we could meet for a drink?"

I almost laugh out loud. The high school Cal wouldn't be seen dead with the old Jenna Warren. But I give him a card and turn to focus on the visitors. When Barb gets back, I laugh and tell her about the conversation with Cal.

"It might do you good to go on a date, Jenn."

It's a busy day but in the slow patches, I think

about her words. Maybe I should start to date again? Thoughts of Dan still linger, but he's thousands of miles away and I need to move on.

* * *

A few days later, Cal calls and invites me to dinner at the most exclusive steakhouse in Boise. After appropriate hesitation, I accept.

I haven't worn the Dorchester black dress since that Christmas Eve. I stroke the material, wishing I was going out with Dan tonight. I sigh and put it on. Time to make new memories.

Barb comes over to see me off.

"Remind me why I'm doing this," I ask as I carefully apply lashings of mascara to make my dark eyes look huge. "We don't mix socially with the Wilsons. Do we even want to?"

"Just see what happens." Barb adjusts my dress a little. "You look beautiful. And you never know, you might convert him to organic farming."

Cal comes over to get me in an expensive car. He wears a beautifully cut suit that perfectly fits his athletic frame and his perfectly sculpted face looks regal in the light of the street lamps as we drive. We make polite conversation in the car about people we knew from school and he escorts me into the restaurant.

It's amazing after years of having had a schoolgirl crush to finally be on the arm of Calvin Wilson. People look up as we walk by and I'm aware of the gossip. I've never mixed in these circles, but Cal is one of the most eligible bachelors in town – and certainly the best-looking. This is also one of the coolest places to be seen and I blush a little at the attention.

But the novelty soon wears off.

For all Cal's good looks, he is only interested in himself. He talks non-stop about how amazing and successful he is. He doesn't ask about my travels or the ranch and I soon tune out. It's so different from the fun and easy conversation with Dan.

I'm relieved when Cal drives me home. He turns the engine off outside the ranch house and I reach for the door, turning back before I go.

"Thanks for a lovely dinner."

He pulls me into his arms, pressing his mouth to mine before I can react. He's probably used to women fainting in his arms, but I push him away.

"I've got to go."

I get out of the car quickly and before he can follow me, I step up onto the deck and let the dogs out. They circle me, barking, delighted at the prospect of a late walk. Cal hesitates, then raises a hand in farewell and drives off. What a relief!

Barb calls the next morning for an update, and I tell her how awful it was.

"Oh, give him a chance, Jenn. He might turn out alright. Your Uncle Doug was pretty useless on our first date."

So when Cal calls a couple of days later, I agree to see him again. I have my reservations, but perhaps Barb is right. I suggest a movie, so I don't have to listen to him talk all evening.

We meet at the Egyptian Theater, recently restored and one of Boise's most cherished, historical landmarks. We laugh at the movie and I even let him hold my hand in the darkness. He doesn't try to kiss me goodnight this time, for which I'm grateful. I realize that it wasn't such a bad evening after all.

Over the next few nights, he calls and we talk about ranching. He's skeptical but at least he listens when I talk about the benefits of organic beef. He shares some interesting ideas and I like that he's as passionate about the ranch business as I am. He's certainly persistent, and I think about the months of silence from Dan. Cal and I have so much in common. Perhaps I should give our relationship a chance?

Chapter 22

I drive in to Boise one morning to pick up the custom saddle for Ellie. The saddlemaker and I finally reached a design that worked and I want to show it to Dad before I ship it to Australia. As I pull into River Point, I'm excited about seeing my first design become a reality. I'm glad I used the last of the travel money to see this project through.

Dad opens the door, I carry the box in and we unwrap it on the dining table with excitement.

The saddle is made from light tan leather with a little chair integrated into it. There are removable sides and the stitching is autumn red. The supportive straps can be adjusted as Ellie grows. I run my fingers over it, a dream become reality. "It's beautiful."

Dad beams, his eyes shining with pride. "You

designed this? I'm so proud of you." He gives me a hug. Then he turns the saddle to look at the back. The name *Warren* is stamped into the leather, entwined with a stylized forest in an oval border.

"I designed the logo, too. Do you like it, Dad?"

"It's great. We should patent this design and then maybe you can sell more of them."

"That sounds like an exciting next step. I love learning about the business side of the ranch, Dad, and designing for special needs is something I care about. It would be great to incorporate it somehow."

Dad makes coffee. "I'm so glad you're taking the ranch business so seriously. Susan and Todd found their own paths and when you went traveling, I wondered whether you'd come back. But you needed a chance to see a different future, if you wanted it."

"Going away helped me realize that I belong here. Thank you for the opportunity, Dad, but I'm a Boise ranch girl from now on." We sit together on the little deck overlooking the lake and sip our coffee. "Are you happy here, Dad? You've been coming up to the ranch less and less in the last month."

"I'm very happy making new memories with Maggie. She helps me live instead of working so hard all the time." He turns to me. "I also want to give you space to make decisions without me and you're doing so well. But remember, I'm always here to help if you need me."

"Thanks, Dad."

I pack the saddle carefully again and take it back into town. As I pay the air freight, I wish I could be there to watch Ellie unwrap it and use it for the first time. Maybe Dan will be there instead? I feel the sudden press of tears at the thought of him and the family in Cairns. Does he ever think of me?

After the package is sent, I go into the café next door, to get a takeaway coffee for the drive back to the ranch. Two girls I once knew from Boise High are sitting in a booth and I stand behind a lattice screen as I wait for my drink. I don't want to make small talk and we were never friends at school, but I can't help but overhear them.

"Did you hear that gorgeous Cal Wilson is seeing Jenna Warren?" one girl says with a flick of her hair.

"Who?" The other one is texting on her phone and doesn't even look up.

"You know, all black hair and long legs. The Warrens have that ranch on the road to McCall."

"Oh, her. Yeah, I know … what about it?"

"Well, Michelle said she heard from a friend that the Wilson ranch is in trouble. Cal is apparently looking to marry into money. The Warren Ranch has excellent land and horses they could sell off."

Her words rock through me. I clutch at the counter, then walk out the door quickly, not waiting for my coffee. Inside the truck, I pound on the steering wheel in anger. How dare he?

I drive back to the ranch and go straight to find Blue. It's a hot day and he's standing inside the cool of the barn. I go to him, resting my head against his flank. He makes a whickering noise of welcome.

"I'll never let anyone sell you, beautiful boy. You are my best friend." He huffs a little and I feel the stability of his companionship. "You're always here for me." I can't help the tears that come now. "I love my life here, Blue, but I'm so lonely. The man I love is on the opposite side of the world and won't speak to me. And here, I'm nothing but a marriage prize with land and money."

I can't seem to stop weeping as I lean against him. His warmth and heartbeat are the only things that anchor me.

"Jenn, you in there?" I hastily wipe the tears from my face as Doug walks into the barn, but he sees that I'm upset.

"What's up, sweetheart? Is it that Calvin Wilson fella you've been seeing?"

I shake my head, but the tears start again. Doug pulls out a clean handkerchief and hands it to me. I wipe my eyes.

"It's not really Cal, although I suppose it kinda is. I heard he's more interested in our land than me. The Wilsons have their eye on the Warren Ranch, maybe the D-Bar as well."

Doug shakes his head. "Imagine what those feed-lot guys would do with this grassland."

I grimace. "Fence everything, burn out the land, use hormones and antibiotics as routine on the stock." I put my hand on Blue. "Sell the horses."

"Doesn't sound like you should have anything to do with him."

"Perhaps marriage wouldn't suit me, anyway." I rub Blue gently behind his ears and he blows sweet hay breath at me. "I've got to be able to escape into the forest and I'm just getting started on ranch management. Maybe I'll stay single, and just love my family and the horses."

Doug pats my arm. "You're strong, Jenn, but Barb and me, we know you're lonely when you take a fews minutes out from working. We want you to be happy with someone who loves you. Just a thought from an old man who cares about you as much as your dad."

I lean over and give him a kiss on his whiskery cheek, then pick up a brush and start grooming Blue, giving his coat a glossy shine with each pass.

"I've never been able to talk to Dad like I can to you and Barb."

Doug chuckles. "Yeah well, you're too much like Greg is why. You need to find an opposite, someone to balance you. I found that with Barb. Finding a true partner is a precious thing, Jenn, worth holding out for."

I can't stop myself and the words come tumbling out. "I think I found someone but then I lost him."

Doug nods. "The English boy, Dan. I know. You mentioned him in your emails, and Barb and I sensed there was more going on."

I keep grooming Blue, so I don't have to look at Doug as he sits down on a straw bale to listen. I tell him the whole story and at the end, he sighs.

"He sounds like a good man, Jenn, and life has a habit of working out in strange ways. Look at your dad and Maggie. Greg never thought he'd find love again." He gets up and pats my arm as he passes. "Don't give up on Dan yet. Wait and see."

* * *

A week later, my phone rings early in the morning. I don't recognize the international number, but as I answer, I can hear excited squealing and cheering in the background.

"Jenna, it's Angie. The saddle has arrived and it's amazing. You are so wonderful to do this. Thank you so, so much."

It's great to hear her voice, and Charlie with the boys in the background. "We're taking it with us to the stables today. We'll make a video of Ellie and Socks and send it to you."

My mind is filled with the memories of tropical flowers and the sound of the ocean. Vivid images of riding along a white sand beach and of being in Dan's arms.

Angie chats away about the kids, what she and Charlie have been up to, then she pauses a moment. "Dan is doing great things at school, but he misses you, Jenna. I'm not supposed to say anything because he thinks it's best for you both to move on. But all the time he's not working he's writing songs, playing music, and missing you."

My heart leaps at her words. "But what can I do, Angie? He won't talk to me or answer my emails."

"We've got school vacation coming up. Maybe you could email him just once more? He's miserable and I sense that you are too. Things might be different this time."

"Thanks so much, I'll try that. Love to you all, and I'll look forward to seeing the video."

She ends the call and the loss I felt when I left

Australia rocks through me again. I walk through our big ranch house and it suddenly feels too big for me on my own. I want to fill it with a family and happiness along with a little bit of chaos, like Angie and Charlie's home. I want the laughter of children in the yard and the thrill of building a future here. I'll swallow my pride and email Dan again tonight. What have I got to lose?

The day flies by with all the usual things I need to do. When I make it back for dinner, I only have enough energy to microwave some stew Barb brought over. I sit at the table eating it, wondering how to phrase my email to Dan, when there's a ping on my phone. My heart thumps when I see the message is from him.

Dear Jenna,

I went to the stables today with all the family and Ellie rode using your saddle. It fits perfectly and I attach the photos. It's a beautiful gift and made my little sister unbelievably happy. You are so thoughtful.

Seeing Ellie's joy today made me realize that life is too short to be without each other and that we should try for happiness somehow. Our school vacation is about to start and I have some money saved. Can I come visit? I miss you.

Yours, Dan xxx

I'm so excited I can hardly breathe. He misses me and wants to come! I don't have to ask him. I hug myself and laugh out loud with happiness. I text back.

Dearest Dan, I miss you too. Please come soon, Jenna xxx

Chapter 23

Two weeks later, I'm at the airport way too early. I drink coffee and stare at the Arrivals board, waiting and waiting and waiting as Dan's flight arrives and takes ages to get through processing.

Then suddenly, the doors open and Dan is here.

I rush into his arms and time stops as we kiss and hug and laugh with happiness. Dan brushes my hair back from my face, his hazel eyes sparkle, looking deep into mine. "I missed you so much, Jenn. I'm sorry we ever said goodbye."

Dan wears jeans with tan boots and a soft brown, checkered shirt under a leather jacket. His bag is hefted over one shoulder.

"Did you buy this especially for Idaho?" I tease him as I rub a piece of his shirt between my fingers and thumb.

"Standard Australian cattle-man gear." Dan grins. "Perfect for a working vacation in Idaho. You said there's a lot of work to do on the ranch."

"You're too pale for the job, even if you're dressed for it," I smile. "You need to be more weather-beaten."

Dan takes my hand as we walk. "I'm in a classroom all day, and you know the Australian sun burns too hot. By the end of the week, I'll be as weather-beaten as you." He leans in to kiss my cheek. "You're incredibly beautiful, Jenna, did I ever tell you that?"

In the truck, we chat about Ellie and the boys, Charlie and Angie, and school. There's so much to talk about and the distance between us melts away. It's like we haven't even been apart.

Dan tells me about his music and how he's started to sell his songs online. "It means I can work from anywhere." He looks over at me, and I sense hope in his words.

We leave his bag in the house and then I take him on a tour of the ranch. Dan asks so many questions that I see everything anew through his eyes and I tell him about how the business runs as we walk around.

"I'm designing saddles now too, and looking at other riding aids for people with special needs."

Dan smiles. "It sounds like things have changed a lot for you since Australia."

We sit on the rail fence at the back of the barn. "I guess I found my purpose, but I needed to go away in order to see that it was right here."

Dan looks up toward the forest. "It's strange because I thought I'd found my purpose in Cairns. But after you left, things to do with school seemed to fade somehow. I want to work with kids, but I also rediscovered my love of music." He takes my hand. "You helped me with that, Jenna." He pauses, then continues, his voice halting. "I wrote you some songs. They're not very good, but –"

I put my finger on his lips. "You wrote songs for me? That's amazing! Why didn't you send them?"

He looks sheepish. "I thought that maybe you'd moved on with your life and found some hunky Idaho ranchman."

I think of gorgeous but boring Cal. I might have tried harder with him once upon a time, but thank goodness, things changed. Now Dan is here and he's all I want. He's my balance and the man I love.

"I can't wait to hear your songs, but right now I want to take you along the Upper Road to meet Mom and Blue."

It's a beautiful day, with bright sun and high white clouds racing on the wind. As we drive, Dan looks out to the mountains in the distance and the Boise River, curving through the valley below.

"It's stunning. I can see why you wanted to come home. And we're not sweating in high humidity, either." He turns and smiles at me, the wind through the open window lifting his brown hair. I see that he means it. He loves my Idaho already, and that makes my heart sing.

I can see Blue and his herd in the distance, but I want to take Dan to Mom's grave first. I wept there for the loss of leaving him, and now he's here with me.

We walk along the little track and I gather Mom's favorite wild grasses. I lay them by her headstone and we sit on the bench to silently read the words.

Rachel Gardiner Warren. Dearly beloved wife of Greg. Adored mother of Susan, Todd, and Jenna.

I lift my eyes unto the hills, from whence cometh my salvation. Psalm 121.

"You must miss her so much." Dan takes my hand.

"I do, but I'm so grateful for the time we had together." I think of Dan's difficult relationship with his mom. "Whenever I sit here, I realize that time is short. We don't know what will happen in life. We need to seize happiness while we can."

I look up into Dan's eyes and time stops. His hazel eyes look deep into mine and he whispers, "I love you, Jenna. I couldn't stop thinking about you after you left. Seeing you here, so confident, so alive …" He shakes his head. "You're an amazing woman."

My eyes fill with tears. It seems so right that we're here together, my mom a witness to the beginning of something new. "I love you, too."

We kiss, and the world melts away. I'm lost in him, in this moment. Then a familiar presence makes me lift my head.

Blue stands on the path, ears forward, watching. I'm suddenly aware of how big he is. He's a stallion, a powerful horse, certainly capable of hurting Dan.

But Dan rises, his palms open. He doesn't make eye contact but slowly turns sideways to Blue and waits, motionless. He's relaxed, and I hold my breath.

Blue huffs a few times and walks down the path, getting closer and closer. He reaches out to touch Dan with his muzzle, sniffing.

Then my wild Appaloosa takes two more steps and puts his head over Dan's shoulder. He's never done that with anyone else but me, and he rests there, completely at ease. It's as if they breathe together.

Dan lifts one hand in slow motion and gently strokes the powerful black neck.

"Hey, Blue," he whispers.

Blue whickers through his nostrils, then saunters

over to me. He bends his head and I touch my forehead to his muzzle, glorying in this amazing moment. Then Blue turns and walks back up the path, returning to his herd.

I go to Dan, and we hold each other. I'm stunned. My best friend, Blue, trusts the man I love and it feels like a blessing.

* * *

The next few days are spent working together on the ranch. I love showing Dan the ropes and I realize how much I've learned since I got back. Sure, I've always done my part, but now, I understand how every aspect of the ranch is run. Dan throws himself enthusiastically into everything, and I love him for it.

After breakfast each morning, we ride out together to check fences, Dan on the big gelding Dad normally rides. I look over at his easy posture.

"You look comfortable on him. Have you missed riding?" Dan edges closer as we circle the top pasture looking for a break in the fencing where some steers broke through yesterday.

"It's great being back in the saddle here with you, where everything is so relaxed and wonderful to be out in the fresh air. I gave up riding at home because

Mum made it such a competitive thing. Here, it's an important part of work on the ranch." He looks out over the fields, his eyes scanning the horizon, looking every inch a cattleman. "Back in Cairns, I took Ellie out to the stables sometimes for her lesson, and her delight showed me what riding could be again." He turns to me. "And here with you, it's just perfect." He stands up in his stirrups, holding onto the saddle horn and pointing. "Is that a break just there, Jenn? By the trees?"

We canter over and dismount, donning tough work gloves to wield wire cutters and tighten the supports. We secure the gap and then Dan wraps his arms around me as we look out across the fields. "I love it here, Jenn."

"I love you being here."

There's so much more to say, but tonight, we're cooking dinner for Dad and Maggie, Barb and Doug. We hurry back to the ranch house and try to decide what to cook.

"I make a pretty good Hawaiian curry," Dan suggests. "How about that? Chicken and spicy pineapple?"

I flick through one of Mom's old cookbooks. "Okay for Dad, me and Barb, but not for Doug. He's a meat and potatoes man, doesn't even eat rice." I stop suddenly, seeing handwriting on the page. "Look at this Dan, my mom's comments on a marinade for barbecue spare ribs. I'll do that, it's Uncle Doug's all-time favorite."

It's strange but comforting to use her cook book. Mom is not here physically, yet she's always in my heart. We drive into town for groceries and I'm reminded of the Christmas Eve shopping trip with Dan. Who would believe food shopping could be such fun?

He gathers the ingredients for his curry and I buy spare ribs. I point out that this store stocks our organic beef as Dan looks over my shoulder at the list.

"I'll find the salad, if you get the pie and ice cream."

We meet back at the checkout line. "Tah-dah!" With a flourish, Dan presents me with a huge bag of baking potatoes to go with the ribs. "Genuine Idaho potatoes, I presume?"

"You presume right."

Keeping a totally straight face, he says in a snooty voice, "But Idaho has a lot more going for it than potatoes," and we crack up with laughter.

It's fun cooking together and we set the table, add candles and napkins, then welcome our guests for dinner. Maggie gives Dan and me huge hugs and Greg shakes his hand firmly, then grins and pulls him into a man-hug as well. A first! Dad is not known for his physical affection, so clearly Maggie is having a positive effect.

"Good to hear how hard you've been working on the ranch, Dan. You're very welcome here."

Barb and Doug arrive and we open beers for the guys and pour ice-frosted Chardonnay for Maggie and Barb. The conversation flows around England and our travels and the ranch dinner goes really well. Our old family house rings with laughter.

Afterwards, when we sit on the deck with coffee, Dan gets out Todd's old guitar and plays us some of the songs he wrote in Australia. The one I like most is about distant love under the stars and hope for the future. I blush as his eyes rest on me while he sings, but I know his flight home is only a week away. I can't bear the thought of being parted again.

How could we possibly make this relationship work? There are two big family rooms downstairs. Maybe one could be converted into a music studio? Maybe Dan might consider coming to Boise to teach? I read in the local paper that the School Boards are crying out for math teachers, and I'm sure Dad would sponsor him for a work visa.

But my dreams are running away with me.

I can't ask him to give up his life in Australia just because I've found my purpose here. And I couldn't bear the rejection if Dan said no. It would break my heart. Perhaps it's better not to dream?

Chapter 24

The next day, Dan sits checking his email over breakfast. He smiles and I ask what's happening.

"There's a message from Ashley. She and Megan are going white-water rafting for a weekend after this break. She wants to know if I'll be back in time to go with them."

Jealousy flares within me as I remember the two bronzed goddesses at the Barrier Reef, their eyes on my man.

"We could go here, if you like?"

Dan nods enthusiastically. "That sounds great. Then I'll be able to compare stories with them when I get back."

I don't want to think of him leaving again, but the time is rushing by. I want us to make some more memories together, so I phone Bill, the owner of the rafting company. Dad and I have rafted with him a lot in the past and there's a trip going tomorrow.

"It should be exciting, Jenna, because the water's high. Most everyone coming is experienced. What about your friend?"

"He's not experienced on white water, but he's physically fit, and is a confident surfer and swimmer."

"He should be okay then, and it evens up the crews across two rafts. See you tomorrow."

* * *

The next morning, we're up early and drive into the National Forest to the river meeting point. "The Salmon is the only big river in Idaho with no dams." I explain. "It runs through pristine wilderness with deep gorges and powerful rapids."

When we arrive, two big rubber rafts, kayaks and all the safety gear lie along the bank. There was a lot of rain two days ago and I've never seen the river this high.

We register with Bill and Frankie, both highly experienced rafting guides. White-water rafting is an extreme sport, so we sign the obligatory litigation waiver.

"You're sure I'll be okay?" Dan asks.

Bill smiles. "Don't worry, it'll be fun. This is the best rafting river in Idaho."

We change into wetsuits with booties and gloves. Even though it's late spring, the water is freezing. Everyone packs their dry bags with clothes and valuables to stow in Bill's Jeep. He and a cook will meet us at the halfway stop with hot beverages and snacks. Dan and I are grinning with excitement as we check each other's safety helmets and life jackets.

Frankie comes over. "Looking good to go. Okay Dan, because of weight balancing, you'll be with Grant in Raft 1. Jenna, you're in Raft 2 with me."

I smile at Dan. "Guess I'll be racing you, then."

He laughs and we join everyone for the safety briefing. Then Frankie directs us to positions in the raft, balancing weight and strength on the two sides.

She points to the river. "Remember, you must respond fast when your guide shouts orders, because the current is strong. Stay alert and paddle like crazy when we say. It's cold and you're going to get wet from the spray. In the unlikely event of the raft flipping, we'll get you out quickly with one of the safety kayaks traveling with us. Just move away from the raft, so that you don't get pulled downstream with the current."

Dan waves as he joins his crew, a wide grin on his face.

"See you at the coffee stop!"

"Let's go."

Adrenaline pumps through my body as we push out from the bank into the shallows. The water is calm in the little bay, but soon, our two blue and yellow rafts with six outriders in kayaks move into the main flow.

I feel the power of the river through my paddle as the white water foams over the rocks. Currents twist in the deep green flow. It's exhilarating, like riding fast on Blue, close to the edge of the wild. I look over at Dan in the next raft. His eyes are wide with excitement as Grant pulls ahead to take them into the first rapid.

Dan braces against the side wall of the raft, pulling strongly against the water with his paddle. Grant shouts instructions as they fight to stay in the middle of the river and angle between monstrous rocks. The water crashes against them, turquoise-green and sparkling white spray. The big raft flexes and I hear Dan hooting with glee, riding it like a bucking horse.

Then our team races through after them. The rapids are almost continuous and we ride the main current, paddling hard as water explodes through the gorge. I lose sight of Dan's raft in a big cluster of rocks and my heart thumps a little harder. But then we're through and he's there, doing high-fives with the rest of his team.

It's not far to the break now, just one more rapid to go. Rafts have capsized here before because boulder stacks cause the current to swirl unexpectedly. With the water this high, there might also be hidden rocks. But Grant is an experienced guide and has run this river many times.

Frankie takes us through a side rapid and we paddle past the other raft, shouting that we might save some muffins for them. We enter the main rapid first, paddling hard through the white water.

The front of the raft rears up as we plunge in, tipping me backward. I quickly throw myself forward again, feet under the straps as levers, keeping my paddle deep in the water.

Frankie shouts instructions. "Left…pull forward! Right side, back paddle!"

I'm panting with exertion as the spray soaks me again. But then we're through!

We all cheer and raise our paddles above our heads, then drift toward the bank. The current eases and we turn to watch Raft 1 come through after us. I gasp as I realize it's being pulled the wrong way.

The spiraling water catches it. The raft flips upwards and over.

The people inside cling on, but as if in slow motion, they tumble into the icy water. There are red helmets bobbing in the water as they emerge.

I try to spot Dan, counting the helmets, but it's hard to see clearly in the froth of water. The kayakers help people get to the shore as the raft continues downstream in the current.

Then I see that two people are still holding onto it.

Dan clings to the side, trying to help an injured girl. He's holding her up, trying to keep her head above water, one hand clutching the raft for support.

"Let go!" the kayakers shout, as they paddle after the raft.

"Let go, Dan!" I scream, trying to make him hear me above the noise of the rushing water. "Let go!"

But it's too late. The raft hurtles into the next rapid.

Chapter 25

The kayakers race after the raft, but it's disappeared into the vortex of rocks and frothing white water. My heart hammers and I watch, helpless, as Dan is swallowed by the river.

Frankie brings our raft into the bank and Bill takes over. She grabs the First Aid bag and runs for a path downstream. I scramble out and hurry after her, slipping and sliding down the embankment.

"Let him be okay," I whisper a prayer. "Please, don't let him die."

As I emerge from the rocks behind Frankie, the kayakers are bringing in a wet girl and an inert body.

"No!" I run to help them carry Dan from the water and lay him on the bank. His lips are blue, his face bloody. But he's breathing.

"Dan, can you hear me?" Frankie kneels by him, fingers on his pulse. His eyes flicker open and he stares around him. His voice is frail and confused.

"Jenna?"

I kneel at his other side, pull off his glove and massage his frozen hand. "I'm here, Dan. You're going to be okay." His teeth are chattering, he's freezing inside the wetsuit. "Can we get his wetsuit off?"

Frankie shakes her head. "We can't move him again until the paramedics get here and check him out. He might have a spinal injury." She unwraps a foil emergency blanket and I help tuck it tightly around him. "We register with mountain rescue when we're on the river. Bill will have radioed for the ambulance. They can't get a helicopter this far, but they'll be on their way. Hang on, Dan."

His eyes close again, his breathing shallow and uneven. I cradle his cold hand in both of mine as he shivers uncontrollably. Guilt washes over me. I shouldn't have brought him on a trip like this. The river was too high and he's not experienced. I was trying to compete with Ashley, my jealousy blinding me to good sense.

Frankie looks at me. "If you want to go in the ambulance with him, Jenna, you need to change into dry clothes."

She nods over to our dry bags that one of the

team has brought down. With a backward glance at Dan's still figure on the bank, I change behind some bushes.

I'm ready when three members of the mountain rescue team arrive with a padded stretcher. One of the medics checks Dan for signs of concussion. She fits a neck collar and nods to the others.

Together they support and lift him onto the stretcher then strap him in tightly. Dan's eyes are still closed and his skin is so pale. For a moment, it's like looking at a corpse and I feel a wave of fear.

"Please be okay," I whisper desperately, as I grab our bags and follow the stretcher.

"Let us know how he's doing," Frankie calls after me.

The medics load Dan into the 4x4 ambulance.

"Can I go in the back with him? Dan's my … boyfriend." The word feels strange in my mouth, but I realize he's far more than that to me now.

The medic nods. "Sure, get in and sit there. Seatbelt on." He makes a nest of blankets around Dan and checks that the straps are tight enough. The ambulance bumps along the track as we drive off.

I lean close, noting every dark eyelash and laughter line on my love's dear face. I want to see happiness there again.

"I'm here, Dan, hold on." I say, softly. "I love you. Please don't leave me."

His eyes open and they are filled with such love. "Jenna," he whispers. "Will you marry me?"

His words rock through me and the answer is on the tip of my tongue. Then his eyes close again and I sit back, wondering whether he was concussed or delirious, or even if I imagined what he said.

We pull up at the hospital. Medics race to the ambulance and wheel Dan inside. The driver helps me down and folds the blankets. "He'll be okay, don't worry. You need to go in to the Admissions Desk. They'll keep you informed."

I stand for a moment outside the entrance, my head spinning. Will Dan be okay? And did he really just ask me to marry him?

I hurry into the hospital.

"Are you family?" The reception nurse asks as I fill in Dan's details on the admissions card.

"I'm his girlfriend."

"Please wait over there. We'll let you know how he is as soon as we can."

I drink instant coffee from a machine and pace up and down, looking up eagerly every time the door opens. I'm desperately worried and see the same concern on the face of everyone in the waiting room. This must be how Dan and Lizzie waited for news of Christine. And now here I am, waiting for news of Dan, my heart ripping apart as I worry for him. Is this what it feels like when you love someone and they are in danger? Part of me wishes I could turn back the clock and be the Jenna I used to be, when life was simpler.

I take a deep breath. No, it's too late. I'm not that girl anymore. And I love Dan. I can only hope that he's going to be okay … and that his words were not some sort of delusion.

The door swings open and a doctor comes in holding a clipboard. "Jenna Warren?"

"Yes, I'm here. May I see him?"

She smiles. "Please come this way. Dan's resting now and he's lucky, there are no major injuries. He's going to be fine."

I breathe a huge sigh of relief and follow her to one of the recovery rooms. Dan is propped up in bed wrapped in white thermal blankets. One cheek has a butterfly bandage, but his skin looks like an almost normal color again. He turns his head as I walk in, and his smile is like coming home.

"Jenna." He reaches out a hand to me from under the blanket. I go to the bed and take it. I never want to let him go again.

The doctor clears her throat. "We want to keep you in for twenty-four hours for observation, Dan.

I'll arrange for a bed and someone will be along shortly to move you. You can stay with him, Miss Warren." She leaves and I lean in to kiss him.

"Dan, I'm so, so sorry. It was too advanced for a beginner."

"It was certainly a memorable date," he says, encouraging me to sit on the bed so we can hold each other. "But it's okay, Jenn. There's no harm done and we have a great story to tell."

I can't help but laugh. "I wanted it to be fun for us, a special memory before you left."

"How about we stick to riding from now on?"

"Sounds like a plan." I reach up and touch his bandage with a fingertip. "Are you really okay?"

He holds my hand. "My head aches and everything will hurt when the painkillers wear off. Tumbling in that current was like being a sock in a washing machine. But everything is right with the world when I'm with you." His dark eyes are suddenly intense. "Jenn, I was conscious in the ambulance and I meant what I said. I can't get down on one knee right now, but I love you so much, and I want us to be together. Will you marry me?"

My head pounds with excitement and I can't help the grin that spreads across my face. "Oh, Dan, yes, of course I will! I love you." He pulls me close and I'm lost in his passionate kiss. When we surface, he holds me close and his hazel eyes look seriously into mine.

"Australia isn't right for me. Cairns, especially. It's too hot and humid. I long for the cool breezes."

My heart sinks and I stare at him. "You mean, you want to go back to England?"

"No, darling girl. I know now what Blue and your life in Idaho mean to you. You're building a future on the ranch. If you'll have me, I want to be here as your partner. Do you remember the story of Ruth from the Bible?"

I nod. "Yes, Ruth goes with her new family to another land."

Dan smiles. "I'll go where you go, lodge where you lodge, and your people shall be my people. We'll be together."

I tuck my head into the curve of his neck, feeling his strong pulse beating against my skin and I know that this is where I belong.

Chapter 26

The next few days are crazy busy. Once Dan comes out of hospital, we make plans for the wedding. He asks Dad for my hand officially, and I'm so happy to see them clasp hands and embrace, accepting each other as family. Maggie and Barb bustle about like mother hens and Doug gives me an approving nod and a wink. All our family members and friends are happy for us, and a wedding here will be like a new beginning for the ranch.

Dan buys me a beautiful turquoise ring. I wear it on a gold chain around my neck for work and on my finger every evening. I even get to flash it at creepy Cal Wilson when we meet him downtown and I introduce him to my fiancé.

But the days pass too quickly and Dan has to go

back to Australia to finish his contract and close down his life there. We talk every day when he's back in Cairns.

"Charlie and Angelina are thrilled, Jenn. Now Ellie is seven and more confident traveling with her wheelchair, so they're all coming to the wedding. Ellie is riding three times a week now and her back is much stronger. Your saddle is helping develop her muscles and her confidence."

I allow myself a moment of pride. "I can't wait to see them all again."

Susan will be my Matron of Honor and supervise the children and one morning, I call Lizzie to ask her to be my Maid of Honor.

"Oh, Jenna. Of course, I'd love to." I hear the smile in her voice. "That's so exciting."

"Of course, Harry is the Best Man."

I expected a shriek of delight, but there is a long silence before she answers. "To tell you the truth, Jenn, I haven't heard from him since San Diego." She sighs. "I don't think he remembers I exist half the time."

"Then this is the ideal opportunity to get you two talking again," I respond cheerily.

* * *

The weeks pass slowly, but there's always work to throw myself into on the ranch and I'm sketching saddle designs in the evening.

After finishing his Australian contract, Dan goes back to Summerfield and I imagine him there.

"Mum thinks I'm home for the college vacation," he says on the phone one evening. "She's very chilled on this medication and is regularly monitored by her doctor. She hasn't mentioned parties at all, just sits watching animal programs and cartoons." He goes quiet.

"What is it?"

"I don't think Mum understands that I'm getting married." I hear the pain in his voice and my heart goes out to him. "I want her to love you, Jenn, but I think she's too far gone."

"I'm sorry, my love. Come home soon."

"Not long now, sweetheart."

I talk to Barb about Christine. She frowns. "If she can travel with her sister, Viv, then of course Christine must come to the wedding of her only son. We'll find a way to make it work."

She offers to have Viv and Christine stay with her at the D-Bar ranch, where Dan, Harry and Todd will also stay the night before the wedding. We find a beautiful rental house with a pool for the Australian family, big enough for Susan and the girls to stay there as well. Then all the kids can be together and make friends. Lizzie will be at the ranch with me, and everyone from out of town will be in hotels downtown. The plans are coming together at last!

One evening at our regular family dinner, Maggie asks me, "What do you want your wedding to be like, Jenna?"

"I have this vision of everybody being happy and Blue carrying me to the ceremony with flowers in his mane and tail." Uncle Doug gives a snort of laughter and almost chokes on his beer. "Poor old Blue. He won't put up with that!"

I stick my nose in the air and ignore him like I used to as a kid. Maggie asks diplomatically, "What does Dan want?"

"He says he'd be happiest in new blue jeans and a Stetson."

Doug recovers after Barb thumps him on the back a few times. He grins at me. "Have to agree with him there, Jenn."

Looks like our wedding will be Western style and I smile to think of our magical day.

"Susan was set on a traditional white wedding," Dad reminisces. "It was a beautiful ceremony in your mom's church, then that big reception down-town. To see you married here will be a dream come true for me."

I give him a monster hug. "Me too, Dad."

* * *

The days pass. Then Dan finally arrives and every-thing is perfect in my world.

"Did you sort out your work visa?" Maggie asks.

"Yep, I'm a Legal Alien. How cool is that? Being married to a US citizen, I'll be able to teach."

I'm going to develop my little saddle business on the side, and together Dan and I will run every aspect of the ranch for Dad. The ranch house is being painted and we're converting one of the bedrooms into his new music studio. I want to make it every bit as special as the studio he had in Summerfield.

We talk about the wedding preparations as we work.

"I researched chuck wagon caterers. I don't want Doug and Barb to work at all."

"Did they protest?"

"Barb did, but in the end, I know she was pleased. The caterers prepare everything and clean up, and they'll be serving D-Bar organic beef for everyone!"

We finish up and go over to the barn where Dad and Doug are supervising the building of a stage at one end. A wooden floor for dancing has been laid over the dirt and contractors are stringing up festive lighting. I hug Dan with glee at the thought of our special day and guide him through the steps of our first dance once again.

He groans as he tries to follow me, protesting with a half-smile on his face. Blue is equally resistant about practicing with the flowers, even with his favorite peppermints as a bribe.

Doug reckons Blue won't be cooperative on the day, not with a hundred strange people watching him.

"He will, if I ask him nicely."

Doug goes off laughing at me and Barb looks up from her list.

"What about you, Jenn? Have you decided on a dress?"

I nod and find the bookmarked page on my laptop to show her. "Lizzie and I looked at Western design, and in the end, I chose this amazing white satin dress with wine-red lacing up the back. Lizzie's dress will be similar but all in a matching wine red. It's one of her favorite colors, too. Both dresses have this scooped front hem so we can wear white leather cowgirl boots. Gotta be able to line dance!"

Barb smiles. "I love the style. You'll both look gorgeous."

I see Dan coming back across the yard so I shut the page quickly and open one showing pairs of cowboy boots. "Can I have the Desperado pair?"

He leans over my shoulder and plants a kiss on my ear.

"Sure." Barb grins up him. "You can wear them for work afterwards and give all the ranch hands a good laugh."

* * *

Lizzie arrives a full week before the wedding and Dan and I take her around the ranch. She exclaims over everything, fitting in right away.

"Oh Jenna, it's wonderful!"

I take her hand. "I want you to meet Blue and we need to practice putting flowers in his mane. I've given up on his tail!"

There are no words to describe Blue, but Lizzie knows horses and I see the appreciation in her eyes. We stand nearby as he and the mares walk down to water. He comes over to greet me and I hold Lizzie's hand in mine for him to sniff. Together, we gently scratch his favorite spot, then I slowly remove my hand and Lizzie murmurs to Blue as she strokes him on her own.

After this, we bring him into the barn every day to practice weaving jasmine flowers into his mane and taking them out again.

"You're so different from last Christmas in

Summerfield," Lizzie says, as she untangles a flower. "I love the special-needs saddles you're designing. Clair from the stables told me to say hi and she's going to be in touch. She's developing their Riding with Challenges program, and is interested in talking about what they need." She pauses and strokes Blue. "I really admire the way you've gone after what you want in life. I need to do that too, but things with Mum …"

Her voice trails off and I go around to give her a hug. "As Doug says, life has a habit of working out in strange ways."

Lizzie smiles. "I guess so. Do you think you and Dan will have kids here?"

I smile at the thought of starting a new generation at the ranch with Dan. "You'll have to be a good auntie and come to visit often."

Blue is dozing now, with one rear hoof bent up, his pose of supreme trust and relaxation. Lizzie returns to braiding his mane. "Yes, I think I'm ready for a change."

I swing the saddle blanket up onto Blue's back. It's heavy white wool with wine-red embroidery but he doesn't even open his eyes. "He's fine with this now. Doug still reckons he won't stay when people start arriving, but I'm sure my boy will do me proud."

* * *

The next day, Dan picks Harry up from the airport. Lizzie and I are on the ranch house steps as they drive into the yard, their heads thrown back in laughter.

"What a handsome pair of men," I say, brightly. "Especially the dark-haired one."

But Lizzie's eyes linger on Harry. His hair and the close stubble on his face are red-gold in the sunlight, evidence of his Scottish heritage. I notice his bright blue eyes and the flash of a warm smile as the boys climb out of the truck.

"Hello, Mouse," Harry says, as he gives Lizzie a hug like a big brother, then comes over to hug me.

Everyone else arrives over the next day or so, and it's a blur of welcoming and catching up. Lizzie's nervous about meeting Charlie, her dad, since the circumstances around her birth and his return to Australia means she's never met him before. But Dan introduces them and Charlie embraces his daughter, wiping the tears from his eyes as he holds her close.

"You're the image of my younger sister, Sheila, who lives in Perth."

It's a happy family reunion. Sometimes, all it takes

is a moment to forget the past and look toward the future.

I catch up with Angelina. We're both apprehensive when Dan's Aunt Viv arrives the night before the wedding with Christine. I'm shocked to see how frail Christine looks. Her hair is still flame red but her eyes are dull. Dan holds her hand and she looks at me without recognition. Part of me is desperately sad that this vibrant woman is now so broken by disease. When Dan comes back downstairs, I see the pain on in his face. I go to him and hug him close. I know all too well the pain of slowly losing a mother.

* * *

The day before the wedding is fabulous, warm and sunny. We all relax over a family barbecue at the D-Bar, while everyone talks and tells stories of other weddings.

Angie and I sit on the deck with Susan and Barb, sipping white wine spritzers. My nieces, Sky and Shelby, carefully wheel Ellie across the yard to feed treats to the horses. The boys are off somewhere with Charlie.

"Where are going for your honeymoon, Jenna?" Angie asks.

"Dan and I need some quiet time together after all the travel. So, we're taking the truck and going south through some of the National Parks, then to LA and up the Big Sur coastline. We'll stay a few days exploring San Francisco before heading home. It should be a fun road trip, stopping wherever our fancy takes us." I turn to Barb. "How is Christine doing at your place?"

"Good. Dan's taken her to visit local sights. Viv is keeping a close watch on things but all seems quiet and calm." She puts a hand on mine. "You don't need to worry, Jenna. I've been taking her out to the barn with me when I groom the horses. It's where she seems happiest."

I tell Dan about our conversation later that night as he quietly plays his guitar on the ranch steps under the stars. It's a gentle song that speaks of family ties, and a love lost and found again. I lean my head against him as we sit together, a moment of calm before our big day.

Chapter 27

Our wedding day is here at last!

It's five in the afternoon and the temperature's perfect. The paddock and barn have been swept and moss green carpet runners laid down. Our country music band is in place, playing quietly as guests are ushered to their chairs in the shade. Lizzie and I watch through knotholes in the barn wall.

"This reminds me of peeping through your spy mirror at Home Farm." We giggle together like schoolgirls.

Next to the white jasmine arch, Dan and Harry are talking to the minister, their black Stetsons held in their hands. They look comfortable in tailored black suits, soft white shirts, and black string ties – a black and white theme to go with my horse. That is, if Blue behaves.

Curious as ever, he comes and rests his head on my shoulder, breathing down my neck. I stroke him under the chin and whisper, "It's okay, lovely boy, you'll be out soon."

The band quietly plays *Another Bride, Another June, Another Sunny Honeymoon* as the final guests are seated. I look at their smiling faces and I take a deep breath. At the end of the aisle stands the man I love best in all the world, and his face is my personal sunshine.

The music changes as Skylar, Shelby and the boys enter in their little Western outfits, pushing Ellie in her wheelchair. All the children have chosen different colored Stetsons and everyone stands to applaud them as they pass.

Blue's ears flicker backward and forward at the sudden noise. Ellie smiles and waves, a miniature cowgirl in her jasmine-covered wheelchair. Apparently, she insists on sleeping with her shocking-pink Stetson.

The photographer moves to position himself opposite the closed barn doors. It's our time to go in.

I talk to Blue as Dad gently slides the saddle blanket onto his back. Blue stands patiently as I mount from a block, sitting sideways and looking forward, one knee curled up as we've practiced. His long mane is brushed into strands like shining ebony and woven with jasmine flowers.

Now that I'm mounted, Doug calms Blue. "The gate's open to the hill, any time you want to go, boy."

I rub Blue's neck and bend to whisper reassurance. Dad stands ready to catch me if I need to jump off, but Blue is steady. Lizzie hands me my bouquet of jasmine and feathery grasses gathered from around Mom's headstone.

"Okay?" At my nod, Doug slowly opens the barn door. The congregation have been asked to be silent at this point, so as not to spook Blue.

"Walk on." I wrap my hand in his mane and Blue bows his head, his neck curving into a magnificent arch. He walks forward into the sunlight. There's a sigh of breath from all the people who see my incredible Appaloosa stallion for the first time. I'm aware of the sweet scent of Mom's grasses, the strength of Blue's powerful body beneath me, and Dan's smile of love as he watches us. Blue is free as the wind, but he chooses to stay with me. Uncle Doug walks by his head, Dad and Lizzie on either side.

At the gate to the paddock, early evening sun shines in heavenly shafts between the branches and we walk in a timeless cloud of gold. Then Blue stops and I feel him tense as we approach the big group of people, too many for my wild friend.

"Enough, Dad," I whisper and he puts his hands on either side of my waist to catch me as I slide down. He presses a kiss on my cheek and I walk to Blue's head, palming two big peppermints into his mouth.

"Good boy."

Distracted by the tangy mints, Blue vigorously tosses his head up and down as Dad slides the saddle blanket from his back. I pass my bouquet to Lizzie and walk Blue to the gate, open to the track and top pasture.

Just before we get there, he shakes and shakes, like a dog coming out of water. A great shower of jasmine flowers explodes all around us and there's a burst of laughter from our guests. Blue kicks up his heels and shoots off, stops, rears, and then bucks all the way to the top of the hill as everyone cheers and applauds. My glorious black and white rocket of a horse gallops free to join his herd. Once there, he looks back, gives a final shake and drops his head to graze.

I close the gate and the band starts up again, this time with a loud and jolly version of *Another Bride, Another June*. All eyes are on the bride again, but I'm so happy that Blue was part of this wonderful day.

I take my flowers from Lizzie with a grin and slip my arm through Dad's. Doug offers his hand to Lizzie as if leading her out to dance and they go ahead of us. Dad and I walk happily down the aisle toward Dan who waits with our minister under the jasmine arch.

We reach him and Dad smiles down at me. "I love you, Jenna." He turns to face my special man. "Take care of my daughter." He places my hand in Dan's. "Jenna is precious to all of us."

"I will, Greg. Jenna is precious to me, too."

I gaze at Dan's face and here we are, together at last. The ceremony passes in a blur, our vows a promise to each other to love and cherish until death parts us. I think of Mom on the hill and know that whatever comes, Dan and I will face it together.

Suddenly the minister is saying that we are married. Dan leans down to kiss me, then everyone crowds around, hugging and congratulating us.

We lead everyone into the barn. The doors are now open at both ends and the evening wind blows through. Straw bales and small picnic tables are placed around the edges, and our cowboy-style waiters serve everyone champagne or soda. The smell of D-Bar beef wafts through the air from the barbecue grill.

After dinner, Dad bounds up the steps onto the stage. He tests the microphone and welcomes everyone to our home in Idaho, the best state in the Union. He welcomes Dan to our family and says lovely things about me that make me blush. Then he raises his glass and proposes a toast to the bride and groom. He beckons me to join him on the stage. I'm nervous at first, but as I look out at the faces of the people Dan and I love best in all the world, I suddenly know what to say.

"Dad, thanks so much. Without you and Maggie getting married, I would never have met the incredible man who is now my husband." I smile at Dan and everyone cheers. "I want to thank Barb and Doug, my second mom and dad, for teaching me so much about ranching and life. And thanks to all our guests, who have come from near and far to celebrate with us." I grip the microphone tightly. "The last party held in this barn was for my graduation and one member of our family was here then, who can't be with us tonight. But she's here in all our hearts. To many of you she was Rachel, but to me, she was Mom. I know that she would love you, Dan." Tears shine in my eyes and he blows me a kiss. "Please raise your glasses in a toast. To Rachel, to Mom."

Everyone stands with me to remember her. Dad holds out his arms and I step into them, burying my face in his shoulder.

"Your mom would be so proud of you today." He pats my back gently.

Dan comes up on stage and I turn to embrace him. Then he gestures to a hay bale at the side of the stage. I sit down and Dad joins me, Maggie by his side.

Dan speaks quietly into the microphone as he picks up his guitar. "I'm not very good at formal speeches but Jenna, I love you and I want everyone here to know how unique and special you are to me. This is my song for you, my darling girl and my new wife."

His voice sweeps me back into memories of a crackling fire in an English cottage, a forest of bamboo in Japan, and a magical ride along the white sand in Australia. He weaves a spell of travel and adventure and ends with the joy of finding our home with each other. As he plays the last chord, I can't help the tears. I go to him and hug him close.

"That was beautiful," I whisper and he kisses me. The crowd applauds wildly.

"I hope it makes up for my terrible dancing," Dan grins and I laugh as I signal to the band. The floor clears for our first dance.

The band starts with a gentle waltz and Dan's arms hold me close. Then, just as everyone is starting to get bored, the beat changes and the band bursts into *Thank God, I'm a Country Girl*. Dan swings me into the middle of the wooden dance floor to whoops of surprise from the guests.

We do the line dance we've practiced together over and over, and it's perfect. Dan does not miss a step. We grin at each other as we stomp, jump, turn and start again. Then Lizzie jumps up, Harry following, then Dad and Maggie, Doug and Barb and everyone else, until our old barn shakes with country music and rhythmic stomping.

The dance ends and everyone hugs us, then the band strikes up another song and the dancing begins again.

Through the crowd, I notice a flurry of commotion near the barn door. Dan's Aunt Viv looks distressed. Dan hurries over and I follow, making my way through our guests. As I reach them, I see his face is stricken.

"She was definitely with me when you sang your song for Jenna," Viv's face is pale with worry. "I was enjoying the line dance and suddenly, she was gone. I'm so sorry, Dan. I only took my eyes off her for a moment."

Dan turns to me and we're suddenly frozen in a nightmare. The sky is darkening outside the barn, and Christine is alone, close to the wild depths of our National Forest. The happiest of days could yet end in tragedy. Dad and Doug, Barb and Harry come over, their faces concerned.

"Christine got away from Viv and disappeared," I explain.

Barb looks grim. "Surely she can't have gone far?"

Dan and Harry jump into a truck to search the Lower Road as Dad and Uncle Doug go to search in the other direction. Dad's hands are tense on the steering wheel, perhaps remembering being out in that forest after Mom died. He takes charge. "Barb, Maggie, can you please keep the party going until we get back with Christine? Jenna, get Blue and check along the creek."

Maggie takes my hand and squeezes it. "Find her quickly, Jenna."

I slip around the back of the barn and can just about make out Blue and the mares silhouetted against the last of the sunset at the top of the hill. I start up the track away from the lights and noise. Lizzie calls out from behind me and runs to catch up. Blue turns his head toward us, but he doesn't move.

"That's odd, he normally comes to meet me right away."

We crest the hill and see the body near his feet, lying against the fence. Christine is curled on her side, motionless, with Blue standing sentinel over her. Lizzie makes a choking sound and runs forward, but I stop her.

"Slowly, Liz. Blue is guarding her. Can you see Dan and Harry?"

Lizzie gulps back a sob. "I can see lights on the Lower Road."

"We need the truck. Can you go attract their attention? I'll stay with Blue and Christine."

Lizzie takes another look at her mom, then runs back. I don't want to touch Christine until Dan gets here, so I go to Blue, speaking softly as I slide my hand up under his mane. He bows his head to mine. "Beloved friend," I whisper against his neck. "Please let her be alright."

Blue puts his head over my shoulder and comforts me. The truck pulls up on the track nearby and Dan sprints over, Lizzie by his side. I lead Blue away. "It's fine now, boy."

Dan kneels by Christine, his face pale as he checks her pulse. There's a moment of silence, then he breathes a sigh of relief. "She's okay."

He wraps his arms around her, and Christine rouses at the sound of his voice . She rubs her eyes like a sleepy child.

"Oh Daniel, I'm so glad you're here. I had the most beautiful dream all about horses. Please could you take me home?"

Dan helps her to her feet and holds her in a long hug. Then he slides an arm around her waist and together, he and Lizzie support her back to the truck. Harry is waiting with the door open.

"I'll walk down, Dan," I call softly. Our eyes meet and understanding passes between us. I know he needs to be with his mom, even on our wedding day.

As they drive away, I stroke Blue's neck. "Thank you for being with me, boy. I needed you today, and so did Christine."

Blue begins to graze and I sit down in the grass next to him for a little while, to think and just be with him. I was afraid after Mom died, and I hid out here on the ranch, trying to keep things as they were. When Dad married Maggie, I was terrified and sure I'd lose him, but their generosity gave me the chance for a journey of my own. Now I've come full circle, back to my home, except that I'm not alone anymore. So much has changed.

Blue alerts me as Dan walks back over the crest of the hill. My best horse friend trusts the man I love and goes on grazing, moving away from us to join his mares.

Dan takes my hand to help me stand and we hold each other close. There's no need for words. Wrapped in each other's arms, we look down on the ranch and our valley together. Dan presses his lips to my hair.

"Barb and Viv have taken Mum back to the D-Bar. The shouting and stomping in the line dance must have been too much for her. She came up here to be at peace with the horses." He looks down at me, his hazel eyes dark with regret. "I'm so sorry that this happened on our wedding day, Jenna. I can't promise that things like this will never happen again –"

I put a finger to his lips. "It's okay, Dan. I understand."

The soft Boise wind lifts our hair, stirring the manes and tails of our horses. Family and friends dance at our wedding celebration below and my mom is near. I feel her blessing upon us as we say goodnight to Blue and walk back down the hill, hand in hand toward the lights and music. There are so many different kinds of love in a human life, and we need them all. But whatever the difficulties in the future, if Dan and I are together, then love will find a way.

Coming Soon:
Love, Home at Last

Lizzie Martin's nickname is Mouse. As a child, she hid in her favorite chestnut tree to avoid a difficult home life, and now, she escapes to her attic room when she's not looking after her increasingly sick mother. She feels trapped in a life she didn't choose.

Harry Stewart is her brother's best friend, a photographer who travels the world, never staying in one place for long. Lizzie has always loved Harry, but he looks upon her as a little sister. They meet again at a wedding in Idaho, USA, and Lizzie wishes her life could be different.

When family difficulties strike and Lizzie loses her home, Harry offers her a job in Edinburgh, Scotland. She begins to build a new life as an artist, finding friends and perhaps, a chance at love. A personal choice expands her horizons, and suddenly Lizzie sees possibilities beyond her broken history.

But when her new life is threatened, Lizzie has to make a decision that will bring her closer to Harry or tear them apart forever.

In this sweet romance, set between Summerfield

Village and Edinburgh, Scotland, can Lizzie and Harry manage to find their home together at last?

Sign up to be notified of the next book in the Summerfield Village sweet romance series, as well as reader giveaways:

www.PennyAppleton.com/signup

Available now:

Love, Second Time Around

Maggie Stewart is a retired environmentalist, working to preserve the heritage of her little English cottage in Summerfield village. Her children have grown and she's content to ride horses in the countryside and enjoy her retirement.

Except she needs money for her renovations – and she's lonely.

When she joins her old environmental team to go up against an oil company intent on destroying a pristine Scottish river, Maggie finds herself working in opposition to a man she once loved from afar, many years ago.

Idaho ranch owner Greg Warren is rich and entitled, with a dark past that he hides behind a professional smile. But inside, he struggles with loneliness after the loss of his wife and the rage of a wild daughter who won't let him move on.

Love blooms as Maggie and Greg take a chance on a new start, but can they find a balance between the two worlds they inhabit?

In this sweet romance, set between the English countryside and the wide expanse of the Idaho plains, can Maggie and Greg find love second time around?

Available now in ebook and print formats.

http://mybook.to/LSTA

About Penny Appleton

Penny Appleton is the pen name of a mother and daughter team from the south-west of England. One of us is a *New York Times* and *USA Today* best-selling author in another genre.

We both enjoy traveling and many of the stories contain aspects of our adventures. Some of our favorite romance authors include Danielle Steele and Nora Roberts, plus we love The Thorn Birds by Colleen McCulloch, as well as Jane Austen and Stephenie Meyer.

Our favorite movies include Legends of the Fall, A Room with a View, and The Notebook. We both enjoy walking in nature, and a gin & tonic while watching the sun go down.

We are good friends … although sometimes we want to strangle each other! Family relationships are at the heart of our books.

Sign up to be notified of the next book in the Summerfield Village sweet romance series, as well as reader giveaways:

www.PennyAppleton.com/signup